I0682641

<u>Willie James Presents:</u>

Secrecy and Deceit

Three Short Stories That Let You Choose Your Own Ending

1

This is a work of fiction. Similarities to real people, places, or
events are entirely coincidental.

Secrecy and Deceit

Book 1. August 25, 2018.

Copyright © 2018 Willie James

ISBN: 978-0692160602

Written by Willie James

Acknowledgments

This goes out to my beautiful wife Elizabeth, my daughter Amiyah, my mother, father, sisters and the rest of my family and friends.

Choose Your Story

Short Story #1: The C.E.O. and the Office Worker

Begins on Page 6

Mike is hired at the prestigious tech giant 'Black Rose Inc' and gets into an intimate relationship with his boss.

Short Story #2: The Best Friend

Begins on page 90

Brittany becomes suspicious of her best friend and husband's relationship after offering her a place to stay.

Short Story #3: The Work Wife

Begins on page 165

Shortly after saying 'I do', Devon develops an intimate bond with a newly hired married woman. He is forced to choose between her and his wife.

Short Story #4: It's Not Mine

Hidden somewhere within this book

Nancy's husband Josh is unaware his daughter isn't his. She slept with his best friend and accidently got pregnant. Telling him the truth means the end of their marriage. She has a tough decision to make.

4

<u>Before You Proceed</u>

Each story is read from the main characters point of view. Every decision made determines their fate. One of the two main story lines contains a happy ending, while the other a shocking twist. Dead ends await you at every turn. They are designed to derail you by placing the main character in a perilous no win situation. Read them all to see how they intertwine with the two main story lines. I've placed reading tips in random locations throughout the book. Use them to your advantage.

A hidden story begins somewhere within the pages of this book. See if you can locate it!

The CEO and the Office Worker

This story has two alternative endings. See if you can find your way past the dead ends to reach them.

Choose Wisely.

Mike is a small town 29 year old man from College Station, TX with dreams of being a professional programmer. Today is his first day on the job with the tech giant *'Black Rose Inc'*. It's practically a dream come true for Mike. He's pretty anxious to start. His alarm clock goes off at 7:00 that morning.

He immediately rushes out of bed. He knows he has to be at the front desk by 9 A.M. and can't risk being late. The company is forty five minutes away from where he lives. The tollway he plans to take is usually packed with morning traffic between 6-8 A.M. That gives him a small arrival window.

Mike makes his way into the bathroom. His appearance is clear once the lights are turned on. Slick waves run across his low fade haircut. His sharp goatee looks freshly cut. His body is of an athletic build. His skin is caramel. He admires how toned his body is becoming in the mirror. His hard work in the gym is paying off.

Mike completes his daily morning routine and surfaces out of the bathroom. His chosen outfit includes a business professional button up white long sleeve with black slacks. Mike races out the door knowing time is of the essence. He manages to beat the traffic and makes it the front desk in the nick of time. Once there, he meets with the same people who interviewed him. A stunningly beautiful woman standing not far behind catches his eye. She's seen conversing with other employees. Her hair is long as it is natural. Her mocha skin and slim curvy body has Mike's mind racing with thoughts of the naughty things he'd love to do with her.

One of Mike's interviewers shakes his hand. He is an older gentleman of Caucasian decent who goes by the name Ed.

"Mike! It's nice to see you again! Glad you can make it on time!" he says.

Mike tries his best to balance conversing with Ed while secretly admiring the woman's beauty at the same time. You see, Mike was a notorious womanizer back in his college years. He has the beautiful lady set as his next target. Ed realizes he has some last minute paperwork he needs to finish processing.

"Hey Mike, can you give me a moment?" he requests.

"Sure."

Ed leaves Mike to finish the paperwork for Human Resources.

The beautiful woman finishes her conversation with her coworkers and is left her standing by herself. The timing couldn't have been more perfect.

Mike's hormones rage every second he sees her in that sexy red dress.

Choose what Mike does next:

Turn to page 11 if Mike waits for Ed to return.

Turn to page 26 if Mike takes a restroom break.

Turn to page 16 if Mike walks over to the beautiful woman and lets her know how much he'd love to sleep with her.

SECRECY AND DECEIT READING TIP:

Will morally correct choices always lead me to the alternate endings?

Of course not. Where's the fun in that? It would be a boring read if you could reach every ending by making a morally correct decision.

Instead of talking to the young lady, he focuses on the bigger picture. He uses his phone to check his social media while patiently waiting for Ed's return. Minutes later, he notices Ed pointing in his direction. Ed just so happens to be conversing with the beauty. She briefly smiles before being interrupted by her coworkers. They tap her shoulder to get her to sign some paperwork. Ed returns to Mike so he can to lead him to his desk. What he reveals is pretty shocking.

"Hey Mike, you see that lady I was just talking to?"

He nods.

"She goes by Kim. She's the C.E.O. of this company. People are in her face 24/7."

Mike's eyebrows rise. He had no idea he was lusting over his boss.

"Anyhow, let me show you to your cubical."

Ed leads Mike to his work station to begin the day. He notices Kim standing in hallway conversing with other staff members. Ed explains a program to Mike that he wants written before the week's end. He distractingly nods while only listening to the keywords. Mike can afford to be distracted. He knows he can complete the program's code within half that time. He's just that good. Besides, he can't seem to take his mind off how attractive Kim is. Mike notices when she disappears into a big office behind the receptionist. Ed shows Mike how to use the Instant Messaging feature on his computer then leaves him to his work.

Mike logs in and finds Kim's name. He playfully opens a chat window and types up a message he doesn't actually intend on sending. He figures there has to be some company policy that won't allow it to go through. She is the C.E.O. after all! He types what's really on his mind.

"You are so beautiful to me. I'd love to take you out sometime."

Choose what Mike does next:

Turn to page 20 if Mike accidently clicks the send button.

Turn to page 54 if Mike exits the window.

Nancy has to get her hands on that test at all cost. It finally arrives a week later. Nancy shreds the paper and empties the trash herself. She then lies to Josh saying the results came back negative. She claims she misplaced the paper when asked to see it. Ten years go by. He notices Dria's facial structure looks very similar to Brian's. He remembers the doctor's suggestion for a DNA test and becomes suspicious.

He notices his wife has called in sick a lot for the past few years when nothing is wrong with her. She's also been very secretive with her phone around him. He leaves work early on a sick day to try and catch her in the act. He ends up walking in on her and Brian having sex. His anger is hard to contain.

Proceed to page 235.

Mike knows he needs an ice breaker interesting enough for this to work. He walks over to the beautiful woman and introduces himself. The ice breaker of choice is a funny pick up line he used in his college years. Before he could get a word out, the lady speaks.

"Hello Michael." she says.

Mike is shocked.

"Wait, do we know each other?"

"I know most of my employee's names. I'm Kim, Black Rose Inc's C.E.O." She responds.

Mike tosses the pickup line idea out the window. For the sake of his job, it's best to keep it professional.

"It's nice to meet you Kim. Hope I can do your company proud."

Mike notices Tina out the corner of his eye standing next to the passenger side door of his car. She knows Mike well enough to be aware of his true intentions with that conversation. After giving her body to him she isn't happy about it. But Mike isn't worried. It's not like they are together right?

Make A Choice

Choose what Mike does next:

Turn to page 67 if Mike cares enough to explain to Tina that it's not what it looks like.

Turn to page 61 if Mike doesn't give a fuck about Tina or her feelings and walks to his car door.

Mike's hormones override his brain. He figures he got a few minutes to spare before Ed returns. Besides, who's to say he'll have another opportunity to get her number? Anyhow, Mike knows a strategy is needed in order to spark a conversation. His sharp eye notices the mini refrigerator next to her. A staff member uses it to get a water bottle out. And thus the perfect excuse to approach her was born. He walks over to the woman while reaching in the fridge.

"Excuse me ma'am."

She looks him in the eye. Her curvaceous body causes an erection in his pants. If they were an item, his hands would be all over her booty right now. He knows he has to behave himself. The sexual satisfaction from exploring her body will arrive in due time.

"Yes??" She responds. It's obvious something is on her mind. It's most likely work related.

"I'm new here and I was told this refrigerator was open to the staff. Just making sure."

"Yes it is." She answers.

Mike proceeds to grab a water bottle. Being blunt and upfront has worked in his favor in the past. He decides to give it a shot, He whispers to her:

"I'm Mike by the way. You are very beautiful to me. If I can be honest, I'm drawn in to how sexy you look in that dress! Your ass looks so soft and firm. I'd love to sleep with you sometime..."

She is taken aback by his boldness. It takes a lot of guts for a man to have that level of honesty with a woman. Mikes gets nervous wondering if he's about to be reported to H.R. or not. Maybe the bold approach wasn't such a good idea. Another man walks up from behind to inform her of a work related problem. She walks away with him to assist. Ed surprises Mike from behind.

"So I see you've met the C.E.O. already! Wonderful!"

"C.E.O.??? Did he really just say..... C.E.O.??" Mike thinks to himself.

He decides to play it cool. In the back of his mind he worries about the repercussions of what he's done.

"Yes. Although I never got her name." he says to Ed.

"Everyone calls her Kim." Ed responds while leading Mike to his cubicle.

So far H.R. hasn't summoned him yet. But he figures it's only a matter of time. Until then Mike avoids drawing attention to the situation. Ed gives him his computer login information and leaves him to his work. Mike begins writing code for Ed's project. About 20 minutes into it, a text message appears on his phone. The number is unfamiliar. The text reads:

"This Kim. 9 P.M. Friday. My place. Don't be late."

Mike can barely focus on his work after a message like that. Even though he's excited, he plays it cool with his response:

"Fo' sho."

She responds with a final message:

"Great, see you then."

And it was over just like that.

Proceed to page 69

SECRECY AND DECEIT READING TIP:

Every dead ending contains a missing piece of the overall story. Reading them all will help you understand parts of the bigger picture. Sometimes they reveal another side to a character that you would've never saw coming. (This can help you in your overall decision making.)

A loud sneeze from a fellow employee causes Mike to accidently click the send button. His heart drops realizing the gravity of what he's done. Mike stares at the computer screen in shock for five straight minutes. That message might've cost him his job. Mike strokes his forehead to mitigate the shame he feels. He begins working, figuring he'll deal with the consequences when they come.

Mike's shift eventually ends. He heads out the door hoping to leave the property long before Kim has a chance to see him. After making it to his car, he high tails it home. Once there, Mike unwinds in his bed. He watches TV until night fall. Shortly after nine P.M. A text message from a foreign number arrives. It reads:

"This Kim from work. I'd love to go out with you but no one can know about it."

Mike couldn't believe what he read. Kim actually said yes! How lucky is he to have the C.E.O. of a billion dollar corporation telling him she's ready to go on a date? Mike responds in his smooth demeanor:

"No problem. There is a small town an hour away from here that has few places we can go."

Kim texts back:

"Sounds like a plan."

Mike begins searching for bars on his phone when another text hits:

"How far do you live away from Indiana Street?"
"Not far at all." He responds.

Indiana Street is surprising close to Mike's apartment. Everyone in the city knows that place is filled with million dollar mansions. The neighborhood is obviously out of Mike's price range. Another text message comes through:

"Call me."

Mike gets a little nervous. He man's up and dials her number anyway. The phone rings twice before Kim answers.

"Hello?"

"Hey, what's up?" Mike responds.

He shakes out of nervousness but hides it well. Kim sounds pretty tired.

"Nothing. It would be nice to have someone hold me tonight." She says.

Mike was out of the bed before she finished her sentence. He can tell she's comfortably lying down in the dark. He searches his drawers for sleeping clothes while trying to keep quiet.

"Oh yeah? Send me the address and I can make that happen." He responds.

"Okay."

She says before hanging up. Her address arrives in his text messages two minutes later. Mike throws on his gym clothes and packs his toiletries. He also takes an ironed work outfit. Twenty minutes later, Mike pulls up to the fancy gated community. The outward appearance has a 'Lifestyles of the Rich and Famous' feeling to it. He knew she had money but wasn't sure how much until now. He drives up to the gate and enters the code she gave him. It opens. Right before entering, Mike realizes he has no condoms. Things could get real messy should a pregnancy occur. He has a decision to make.

Choose what Mike does next:

Turn to page 33 if Mike heads to the store to pick up some Trojans.

Turn to page 24 if Mike wants to experience her raw.

Turn to page 35 if Mike decides to rob her.

Mike knows why he needs a condom from a protection standpoint. But it's almost 10 P.M. and he is on his way to his bosses' house while hard as a rock. Logical choices are being suppressed by his hormones. Right as he pulls up, Kim steps out her front door. She walks over to the driver's side window and speaks.

"Let's go to the gas station. I want to pick up some wine." She says.

Mike knows that's code for *"In case you forget the condoms."*

It looks like raw sex with her is off the table after all.

Mike and Kim exit the neighborhood and notice a gas station on both sides of the car nearby. Mike randomly pulls into the one on the passenger's side. The cashier, whose name is Sarah, instantly recognizes them both. Kim is horrified at the sight of her. She knows Sarah's the same woman who works the registration desk during the day.

"Hey Kim! Mike! What can I do for ya'll?" She asks in a friendly tone.

"Sarah…hey." Kim nervously responds.

Unbeknownst to Kim, Sarah also works a second job at the gas to help pay for school. She remembers Mike from checking in for his initial meeting with Ed earlier.

"Looks like your first day is going pretty well." She jokes. Mike is in no laughing mood. He knows how damaging this could be for the both of them. It doesn't take long for word to spread bout Kim and Mike's corner store run the next day. Kim Is forced to step down as C.E.O.

Mike is immediately fired. Without a job, his bills begin to pile up. He has a hard time finding another to stay afloat. He eventually gets evicted out of his apartment and is forced to live in his car.

You reached a dead end.

Make another choice on page 23

Mike decides to take a restroom break. He uses the excuse to get a better look around the place. After coming out the men's room, he returns to the front desk. The beautiful lady disappeared. He looks around for Ed and sees no sign of him either. He browses the internet on his phone to kill time. Suddenly, he gets a text message:

"Hey, this Tina. I didn't realize you also work at my job!"

Tina? His ex-girlfriend from two years ago Tina? Mike remembered how fine she was. Their love making sessions were some of the passionate he ever felt.

"But how did she see me?" Mike thinks to himself. Another text comes through:

"Meet me in C104 ."

Mike is soon interrupted by Ed's return. He shows him to his cubicle and gives the whole spill about what the company expects from him. Mike nods while thinking about sneaking off to C104 to meet up with Tina.

"I was hoping to introduce you to the companies C.E.O. Kim, but she looked pretty busy earlier."

"Is that who we saw standing across the room earlier?" Mike asks.

"Yes, that was her. She's a very busy woman. I'll introduce you two at some point."

Ed eventually leaves Mike to his work. He types up a few lines of code to stall time. Mike eventually rises from his seat and exits the room. He roams the buildings main atrium until stumbling upon a sign that reads 'C-Wing'. He goes down the hallway and quickly finds room 104. He wonders if Tina is truly on the other side of the door.

Suddenly it props open. Tina peaks one eye through the crack and signals for him to enter. Mike doesn't hesitate. He finds himself face to face with her in a small broom closet. Mike pretends to not know why he's there. In the past they made love on the job all the time. This move was nostalgic for them both. Before Mike could get a word out Tina removes her panties.

She then drops to her knees and gives Mike oral sex. He enjoys the euphoria feeling Tina's mouth gives him for a few minutes. She eventually rises to get in doggy style position. Mike knows he doesn't have any condoms on him right now. Pregnancy is definitely not in the cards either.

Choose what Mike does next:

Turn to page 30 Mike decides to have sex anyway.

Turn to page 29 Mike isn't risking a pregnancy and says he has to go.

Mike can't risk getting Tina pregnant. He zips up his private and backs away.

"Sorry Tina, But what we had is in the past. I can't go there with you. I have to go!" He says trying to let her down easy.

Tina isn't the type to take no for an answer. Feeling rejected, she responds by saying

"You telling me you don't miss this?"

Mike won't admit it but he does miss the feeling of being inside Tina's warm vagina. It's something about her craziness that enhances the experience. She reaches in his pants and starts playing with his private area. His common sense is being overwritten by his hormones. The more she strokes the tip the more Mike gets into it. He eventually loses control of himself and turns Tina back around.

Proceed to page 30

Tina holds herself up against the wall as Mike penetrates her vagina for another 10 minutes. He finishes inside her and is immediately overcome with regret for not using protection. She puts her clothes on while preparing to exit.

"Is your number still the same?"

Mike nods while making sure his belt is secured.

"Cool. I'll text you when I get home."

She heads out. Mike returns to his desk trying to forget about the whole ordeal. His shift ends eventually. He makes it to the parking lot and notices the beautiful woman from earlier also walking to her car. She is alone. Mike knows this is a golden opportunity to talk to her.

Proceed to page 14

Mike decides to do the right thing. He tells Tina he can't do it without any condoms. Tina is offended.

"So...You're just gonna up and leave?"

Mike now realizes why they are no longer together. Tina has a dark psychotic side. He returns to his desk. She sends twenty texts messages back to back demanding he return; he ignores them all. She eventually stops. Mike assumes she gave up. Two hours later, Ed shows up with two police officers at his desk. Tina stands behind them appearing visibly shaken. Ed speaks in a stern yet disappointed voice.

"Mike, Your services are no longer needed."

Mike looks at them in confusion.

"Did I do something wrong?"

Mike notices Tina's constant weeping behind the cops. She's putting on the performance of a life time. She claims Mike forced her into that closet and raped her. Mike is handcuffed and taken to jail for a crime he never committed. Weeks later, he gets a court appointed hearing. Tina shows up and continues her Oscar worthy performance. She manages to get the Jury to believe her rape accusations. He gets sentenced to ten years in prison. Tina also files a restraining order against Mike to make her story more believable. The order prevents him from being within ten yards of her.

You've reached a dead end.

Choose a different path on page 47

Mike decides to head out to get condoms from the gas station. He'll let Kim know that he's in the area once he returns. He pulls into the closes one on the driver's side and buys the Trojan brand. Mike then returns to Kim's house and fires off a text:

"I'm here."

Seconds later, Kim opens the front door. Mike enters the house only to witness how attractive her body is in a silk robe. Every light in the house is off with the exception of a lamp in the master bedroom.

The chills from the cold air conditioner force Kim back into bed. Mike heads into the bathroom to change into his night clothes. He then makes his way into her bed and holds her. Kim feels the warmth of Mike's body. Her soft booty lies gently against his pelvis. He feels his erection rise. No words are exchanged between them, only cuddling. Kim starts to fall asleep. Mike lets his hands caress the curves of her body. She feels his erect penis gently stroking her booty. It eventually finds its way to her vagina. He inserts himself in. The warmth and euphoric feeling her vagina brings causes Mike's body to go numb. Kim arches her leg up to allow him more room to stroke. Before going any further, Mike puts on a condom. He no longer feels he has to hold back in any way. Mike flips Kim on her back and continues to have sex with her. The cold air is drowned out by the heat their bodies produce. They alternate between sleeping and having sex for the rest of the night.

Proceed to page 38

Mike admires the size of Kim's house.

"Why work 40 hours a week for pennies when people like her are making millions off our labor?" he contemplates.

Mike's been laid off before. There's also no guarantee that Black Rose Inc. won't go bankrupt in the future. And even If it does Kim will still be rich. He knows he has to look out for himself. Mike's believes Kim may have a safe filled with money somewhere in her mansion. He's determined to find it. He discreetly parks around the corner and sneaks into her backyard. Even at night he's amazed at the view.

Kim's swimming pool looks like something out of a waterpark. Beach tables and chairs are placed around it. L.E.D. lights within the water make a midnight swim inviting. Mike keeps his eye on the prize. He strolls to the back door and rams into it with the force of a swat team. Kim lets off a terrified scream from within. After three tries, Mike breaks the door down. He ends up in the kitchen. He sees Kim trembling on the phone with authorities while racing towards the master bedroom. Mike runs at full speed trying to catch her like a psychopath out for blood. She slams the door shut. He barely misses her by a millisecond.

"KIM, THIS ISN'T PERSONAL! I JUST WANT THE MONEY!" He yells.

Mike knows he can't leave empty handed. He'll be unemployed once this is all over. Mike rams the bedroom door with all his strength. The integrity of the wood begins to crack. Kim's screams are heard on the other side.

"MICHAEL DON'T MAKE ME DO THIS!" She yells.

Her words fall on deaf ears. Mike is already thinking of an escape plan. He eventually breaks the door down.

"ENOUGH OF THIS SHIT! TELL ME WHE-". He yells before noticing Kim aiming a .45 caliber handgun at him from across the bedroom.

Seconds later, she lets off a few shots. Mike is hit several times in the chest and dies instantly. His lifeless body drops to the ground. Police sirens get louder outside signaling they've arrived. The story hits the local news station days later.

Dead End

You've reached a dead end.

Make another choice on page 23

The next day arrives. The alarm clock goes off revealing its 7:00 in the morning. Mike awakes to see Kim in the restroom prepping for work. He makes his way into the bathroom. Kim smiles while fully dressed in her work attire. Mike only has his boxer shorts on at this point.

"Good morning handsome."

"Good morning. What time you heading to work?" he asks while jumping in the shower.

Kim returns to applying her make up.

"Probably in another hour." She responds.

They finish their morning routines and spend the remaining time cuddling on the couch. They both are watching the news. The time to leave for work arrives. Both Kim and Mike head to their cars. They know their current situation isn't something that can be publicized.

"It's going to be weird pretending we don't know each other." He says.

His response reassures their privacy. Kim smiles while entering her car.

"I'll text you later." She says before closing the door and driving off.

Mike cranks the engine and heads to work himself. Once there, he heads to his cubicle. Ed shows up as soon as he logs in his computer.

"Mike my boy! How you liking the job so far?" he asks.

"I love it here. Wouldn't trade it for the world." Mike responds.

"That's great to hear."

Mike's mind visualizes Kim's soft booty throughout their conversation. He can't wait to see her again. Ed branches off work topics to talk about a recent camping trip he took his family on. Mike can see himself hitting a bar after work with Ed one day. As much as they are enjoying the conversation, they know they must get back to work. Ed says one last thing before walking off,

"I had a meeting with Kim yesterday. She feels you are perfect for the company."

Make a choice

Choose what Mike does next:

Turn to page 41 if Mike says "I was perfect for her bedroom too."

Turn to page 43 if Mike returns to his work.

Mike feels he can tell Ed anything. He signals for him to lean in closer. Ed complies. Mike then reveals the unthinkable.

"Last night, her bed was a perfect fit for me too."

Ed looks surprised.

"Wait, what? You slept with her?"

Mike nods with a smirk.

Ed responds by walking away silently; leaving him to ponder what went wrong. He's about to learn why you shouldn't trust coworkers with your personal business. An angry text message from Kim hits his phone:

"You told Ed about us?????"

Mike's jaw drops. He knows he fucked up big time. One of the company's golden rules prevents supervisors from being involved with their subordinates. As expected, Ed returns with a request to immediately see Kim in her office.

Once there, Mike lies to protect Kim's reputation. He says he made the whole thing up. Kim has no choice but to terminate him on the spot. After the meeting, He shamefully walks back to his car.

Guilt completely distracts Mike while on the road. He blows through a stop sign and gets into a major accident. It paralyzes him from the waist down. He spends the next 10 years learning how to walk again.

You've reached a dead end.

Make another choice on the previous page 40

Mike ends the conversation by returning to work. He writes the background code for a program that creates work orders and assists with task management. Even though it's complex, Mike knows it's nothing he can't handle. By lunch, he has a working prototype.

Mike visits Ed's office to show the project is near completion. Ed is thoroughly impressed at how quickly he works. He schedules a meeting in the company's conference room to show off the prototype to the other high level execs, including Kim. During the meeting Mike gets the surprise of a lifetime. One of the execs happens to be his ex-girlfriend, Tina.

"It's nice to see you again." Tina says while giving him a soft hug before taking her seat. Kim's face has skepticism written all over it. She turns to Tina.

"I was unaware you and the new hire knew each other." She says to her.

Tina smiles.

"We're old college buddies. I remember Mike was the smartest kid in our class."

Tina is of course down playing their relationship. They use to have plenty of wild sex back when they were together years ago. He stands in a room with his new play thing and his ex at the same time. Who could've seen this coming?

All the execs sit at the conference room's round table. Mike stands by a giant monitor with the prototype software displaying. He feels awkward talking professionally with Kim as if they didn't just have passionate sex the night before. She doesn't break character. Mike's presentation goes well. Everyone is thoroughly impressed with what they see.

You're on the right path.

Proceed to page 45

Mike finishes his presentation and receives a standing ovation. He takes a seat at the conference table shortly after. Tina congratulates him before speaking about the company's recent increase in customers. Kim looks as if she's paying attention. Mike receives a text message that says otherwise:

"Just old college buddies huh?"

Mike notices Kim never breaks her professionalism.

He sneaks a playful text back:

"Jealous? Lol. I never knew she worked here."

Kim briefly looks at her phone. She looks back up seconds later when Ed asks about the budget. She manages to sneak a playful response mid conversation. It hits Mike's phone:

"She's been here for a year. Staff members usually complain she's being a bitch."

Mike takes it as a challenge to break Kim's professional demeanor. He knows it won't be possible but will be fun trying. He aims for a smile with his next response:

"I'd be a bitch too if I had to wear that weave on my head all day."

Mike keeps a straight face though he's dying laughing on the inside. Kim glances at her phone before carefully positioning one hand in a curious posture over her mouth. Her elbow resting on the table gives the appearance that she's listening to Tina. Mike can tell he succeeded. Kim sneaks another response out to his phone:

"Lmao I'm not finna play with you today."

Eventually the meeting ends. Everyone rises ready to exit the room. Mike gets endless compliments about the wonderful job he's doing.

"It hasn't been a week and you're already making us proud!" Ed boosts. Tina smiles while walking towards the door.

"Keep up the good work Michael!" Kim says while walking out the room. Ed is not far behind. Being the last to exit, Mike turns out the light then proceeds to close the door. Tina quietly pushes him back in and closes the door. She shushes Mike by placing a finger over his mouth. They head to the only closet in the room. Tina speaks softly into his ear.

"Damn daddy I missed you."

Even though she's turning him on, Mike knows in his heart he can't do this. His world will end if Kim finds out. Tina is already unbuckling his pants.

Choose what Mike does next:

Turn to page 31 if Mike declines after realizing he has no condoms.

Turn to page 51 if Mike lets her have her way with him.

Turn to page 48 if Kim joins in on the fun.

Mike decides not to ignore the sexual desires Tina awoke inside him. He passionately kisses on her neck and doesn't hesitate to pull out his private. Tina can feel the penetration from behind. Mike closes his eyes and allows the pleasure of her vagina to overtake him. He starts with a soft thrust and gets rougher the more they get into it.

Unbeknownst to them, Kim's office is on the other side of the wall. She notices a faint noise coming from it. She decides to investigate it. Once the conference room door opens, Tina and Mike freeze. They're aware someone's outside the door. What if a meeting is about to commence? That means they'll be stuck until it's over. Kim suddenly flings the door open exposing the two inside. She notices their privates are out. Mike and Tina fear this might cost them their job.

Kim and Mike awkwardly stare at each other for the next 10 seconds. She turns and heads for the door.

"Wait, I can explain!" Tina pleads to Kim.

Instead of walking out, Kim shuts it. This leaves Tina and Mike surprised. Kim gets in the closet with them without saying a word and closes the door. Tina and Mike are beyond confused at this point. Kim gently pushes Mike back to the wall and begins undoing her pants. Mike lets off a big smile while unzipping his pants.

"I've always wanted to know what a threesome was like." Kim reveals. They have quiet sex for the next hour. Six days later, they agree to be in a polyamorous relationship. Kim allows everyone to move in so they all can be together. Their happiness is short live. Tina realizes she is more into girls and wants an exclusive relationship with Kim. She tries to convince Kim to agree to leave Mike. Kim just doesn't see herself going full blown lesbian and refuses. This drives Tina off the edge. Mike becomes an obstacle preventing them from being together. Tina develops a plan.

It's her turn to cook dinner one day. Mike's pretty thirsty from working out earlier. Tina slips poison in his drink before giving it to him. Mike immediately drops his glass after being overtaken by a dizzy spell. The spell gets worse, causing him to stumble away from the kitchen table. Kim helps him lie down on the floor.

Tina pretends she has no idea what's happening and calls 911. Kim fights to keep him conscious. Mike dies minutes after the ambulance arrives. Even after that, Kim still refuses to get into a lesbian relationship with Tina.

You've reached a dead end.

Make another choice on page 47

The C.E.O. and the Office Worker

Alternate Ending #1

Since they messed around in the past, Mike lets her have her way. Kim's phone conversation is heard from the other side of the wall. Mike can barely make out her words yet can tell the call is important. It's a mistake to continue sleeping with Tina. He decides to let her down easy.

"I'm sorry, we can't do this." He says.

"I just got this job and don't want to do anything that will put it in jeopardy."

Tina appreciates the maturity of his response. She then puts her clothes back on.

"That's fine. I totally get it." She responds to him.

Mike checks his clothes before exiting the closet.

"Look Tina, I think you are a very attractive woman. You work a very high level position at a billion dollar corporation. That isn't easy by any means. You are worth way more than a quick closet fuck with an ex. Let's keep it professional."

Ashamed, Tina grabs her purse and leaves without saying a word. Mike returns to his desk as well. The man in him wants to slap himself for turning down sex with her. What other man does that?

Mike returns to Kim's house later that night. After another sexual experience, he gets invited over every day. What started off as a one night stand evolved into a full blown relationship. Mike quits his job a little after a year passes. Kim is curious as to why. He shows her by getting on one knee.

"God told me not to let anything stand in the way of making you the number one priority; I'm taking a chance on you." He proposes to Kim.

Kim cries joyful tears while he continues.

"I will gladly trade my dream career for your hand in marriage any day."

They both wed and announce a pregnancy that same year. Kim gives birth to a beautiful baby girl 9 months later. She helps Mike start another technical business shortly after. It goes on to gross over one hundred million within the first two years.

Return to page 9 and see if you can find your way to alternate ending #2.

Mike exits out the window. He resumes working on all of his assignments. A few hours later Mike sets out for lunch in the lobby. There, he sees Kim putting quarters in a vending machine waiting for the snack to drop. It's the perfect time to strike up a conversation. He heads to the neighboring vending machine while pulling out his wallet.

"Kim is it?" Mike says while holding up a dollar.

"Yes it is. Welcome aboard." Kim smiles.

"I hear you do good work. I'm glad I recommended you pass to the interview phase."

Mike's eyebrows rise.

"Oh really? Well I'm definitely thankful for the chance to write code for a living. This is the opportunity of a lifetime for me."

Kim smiles while heading back to her office.

"I look forward to seeing more of you, Michael."

Mike, being the smooth man that he is, goes for it. He doesn't let nervousness stop him.

"I'd love to see you this weekend. Coffee perhaps?"

Mikes heart races. Kim says nothing in response. She simply walks away smiling. Mike feels rejected. Oh well! It's better to live with no regrets he figures.

Moments later, Mike receives a text message from a foreign number.

"This is Kim. I'd love too."

Mike can't believe it. The company has a policy against dating employees, but she still wants to go out with him. Mike feels an overwhelming joy. He returns to his work desk to finish a program Ed emailed him about earlier.

The more Mike codes the more he realizes how wealthy the software could make him. This one in particular is designed to help patients keep track of their daily medication. Mike soon develops thoughts of stealing the code for himself. It could easily turn him into a multimillionaire.

Make a choice

Choose what Mike does next:

Turn to page 58 if Mike steals the software for himself.

Turn to page 60 if Mike decides to play by the rules.

Even though Mike is really into Kim, he can't bring himself to delete Diamonds number. Thoughts of feeling her soft booty grind on his dick drives him to make a bad decision. He has to experience her at least once. It's been decided. He's going to see her.

Proceed to page 71.

Why should someone else get rich off his hard work? After his shift ends, Mike downloads the software on to a thumb drive then heads home. He sees Kim walking towards her Mercedes Benz. Her smile acknowledges him before getting in. Mike does a slight wave while smiling back.

He gets back to his apartment and downloads the software onto his personal laptop. He feverously continues writing until midnight. After finishing, Mike phones an old college buddy with heavy ties in the city. With the proper funding secured, he could be the head of his own billion dollar empire. The friend promises to make a few calls when he can. He gets back to Mike the next day. He was able to find a private investor interested in the project. It doesn't take long for the company to get off the ground. It becomes an overnight success. Mike quits his job to run it full time. The company then goes on to generate half a million dollars within its first month of operation. Unfortunately, Kim hits them with a lawsuit after finding out about the stolen software. Black Rose Inc. had the idea patented long before it reached Mike's desk. The judge puts out a cease and desist order to halt production. He has to pay 100% of his profits over to Black Rose Inc. Mike is left jobless and broke. Neither of his ex-business partners take his calls.

You've reached a dead end.

Choose a different path on page 12

Make another choice from the previous page 56

As lucrative as this software would be, Mike knows it isn't right. He continues to work on the project at hand. Completing it will elevate him to a higher position within the company one day. Mike eventually finishes and turns his work over to Ed.

Mike is shocked to find out Ed quits that same day. Mike's not the only one who saw the software's potential. Ed re-releases it under his own company. He becomes a millionaire overnight courtesy of Mike's hard work. Kim sues Ed and causes the downfall of his business.

A few weeks later, Mike and Ed run into each while shopping at the supermarket. Ed nervously greets him. Mike responds with a fist fight. Ed defends himself by stabbing him in the chest. This sends Mike to the ER. The doctor reveals a vital organ was punctured. He will be on medication for the rest of his life as a result.

You've reached a dead end.

Choose a different path on page 12

Make another choice from the previous page 56

Mike doesn't give a fuck about Tina or her feelings. She cheated on him with a football player back in college. He continues on to his car while ignoring Tina. She refuses to let him pass without a fight.

"I know I didn't see my man talking to another woman did I?" Tina snaps at him.

This leaves Mike baffled. Has Tina lost her damn mind? Why does she think because they had sex they are now in a relationship?

"Your man? What are you talking about!?" Mike asks.

"You must think I'm some cheap hoe! You became my man the minute you entered my pussy." Tina says back.

Mike laughs before responding.

"Tina, it's late. You need to go home. You sound real delusional right now."

He proceeds on towards his car. Tina gets in his face before he could reach the door.

"You no different from these other sorry mothafuckas out there. All they wanna do is fuck."

The more Tina rants, the crazier she sounds.

Choose what Mike does next:

Turn to page 65 if Mike tells Tina "Maybe you should stop fucking every dude you meet."

Turn to page 63 if Mike tells Tina "If you don't get your ugly weave wearing ass the fuck out my face?"

Mike decides to be petty.

"I don't have time for this shit, move!" Mike demands while reaching for his car door. Tina gets back in his face. He's getting more agitated with every second passing.

"Look bitch! If you don't get your ugly weave wearing ass the fuck out my face!" He yells out of anger.

Tina responds accordingly.

"OR WHAT? WHAT THE FUCK ARE YOU GOING TO DO? YOU POOR EXCUSE FOR A MAN!! "

This goes on for another five minutes. Tina eventually storms off. Mike is finally able to get in his car and head home. He flops on the couch hoping to replace the encounter with Tina with television. Out of nowhere Mike gets a call from Ed.

Tina used her company credentials to change Mike's password and logged into his email account. She secretly recorded their sex session without his knowledge. She sent everyone in the company a link of the video, all through his account. Needless to say they are both terminated the next day. Nine months later, Mike receives a letter from the child support office explaining why his wages will be garnished.

Tina got pregnant and gave birth to a baby boy. She put Mikes name down as the father. He immediately requests a DNA test revealing he did in fact father her son. They spend the next five years battling over custody right.

You've reached a dead end.

Choose a different path on page 9

Make another choice on the previous page 62

Mike's heard enough. He decides to give Tina a piece of his mind.

"You're the reason we aren't together anymore! Remember, YOU CHEATED ON ME WITH A FOOTBALL PLAYER!"

Tina is offended. He continues to spew venomous words at her.

"BY THE LOOKS OF IT, HE HIT AND QUIT YOUR CRAZY ASS TOO. MAYBE YOU SHOULD STOP ACTING LIKE A HOE AND FUCKING EVERY DUDE YOU MEET! MAYBE THEN YOU'D FIND A DECENT MAN!"

Tina storms off, but not before cursing him out one last time.

"FUCK YOU ASSHOLE! YOU'RE SO GOING TO REGRET THIS!"

Needless to say, Tina followed through on her promise. Ed's house mysteriously gets burned down. Several of his neighbors' homes are also caught in the crossfire. Two people died and ten injured as a result. Ed is confirmed to be one of the deceased. Mike's DNA is found on the scene, though he was nowhere near it.

Shortly after a court hearing, he is charged with Arson along with capital murder of the first degree. They give him thirty days to begin his sentence. Two weeks later, the cops discover Mike has fled the country. Even though he's innocent, he knows it'll be an uphill battle trying to prove Tina set him up. Mike can't risk spending life in prison. He's forced to live overseas as a fugitive.

You've reached a dead end.

Choose a different path on page 9

Make a difference choice on the previous page 62

Mike doesn't feel responsible for Tina's feeling. He tries to let her down in a way that's easy to take.

"Look Tina, first off I'm thankful for the good time back in the broom closet."

Intrigued by his words, She allows him to finish uninterrupted. Mike continues.

"But truthfully you don't want me as a boyfriend. I know I'm going to lust after other woman. You deserve someone who is ready for what you want right now."

Tina thanks him for his honesty.

"You are the first man who kept it real with me."

He continues to tell her everything she wants to hear. Eventually the conversation ends. They briefly hug before Tina heads to her car. Mike lets off a huge sigh. He's happy to have gotten rid of her.

Mike returns to his cubicle to work on more coding. Tina gets back to her management duties. One day, Ed informs Mike of an out of state trip he is required to take. A customer purchased software from the company recently and needs help getting setting it up.

Tina is also required to attend to answer any sales questions they may have. Mike arrives on a different flight due to scheduling issues. After landing, he learns about Tina's plane stalling in the sky and crashing into a mountain. He feels guilty for using her for his own sexual desires. The guilt surfaces in the form of an alcoholic addiction. Mike attends weekly counseling sessions to help cope with the pain.

You've reached a dead end.

Choose a different path on page 9

Return to the previous choice on page 15

Friday arrives. Mike races home to prepare to stay at Kim's house. They haven't seen much of each other throughout the week. Her calendar was filled with meetings. After getting out the shower, Mike receives a text from her.

"You still coming over?"

Mike doesn't hesitate to respond.

"Yep. I'll be there at 9."

Mike throws on overnight clothes. He brings a casual outfit should they decide to step out the next day. After getting ready, he heads in her direction. He soon finds himself in front of her house.

He pulls up in the driveway, amazed at how massive it is. It's obvious Kim is a multimillionaire. Mike sprays cologne on himself and heads to the front door. The door opens before he gets a chance to press the doorbell. Kim answers completely naked. Mike is immediately turned on.

"Wow, you look...amazing." He says while entering the house. All lights are off except a lamp in her bedroom. Mike follows her into bed. After turning off the lamp, the only source of light comes from her phone. Kim suddenly remembers something.

"I forgot to start the washing machine. I'll be back. Feel free to get comfortable." She instructs Mike.

He knows get comfortable is code for get naked and complies. He lies awaiting her return. He notices her unlocked phone on a night stand with her wallet sitting next to the bed. It would be nothing for him to take a peak.

Choose what Mike does next:

Turn to page 72 if Mike goes through her text messages.

Turn to page 82 if Mike goes through her wallet.

Mike decides to go to the strip club to see Diamond. Why not? He figures. After arriving at *Fantasy's,* he pays to get in. Mike then lets Diamond know that he's arrived via text. She responds with "K."

He spots her completely nude entertaining another customer after walking in the door. He takes a seat and waits for her to finish. She eventually finds her way into Mike's lap, offering him a dance. He accepts.

Diamond slowly grinds on Mike while he tucks a few twenty's in her thong. She asks if he wants to go into the champagne room upstairs to have some privacy. Mike happily agrees knowing exactly where it will lead. Diamond takes him into a private room. They talk for a few minutes before having sex. She surprisingly doesn't charge him anything for their encounter. Mike wonders why.

You're on the right path.

Proceed to page 87.

Mike is curious to see those text messages. He quickly leans over and scrolls through them hoping to find evidence of other men. Mike doesn't like his women to have too many bodies on them.

A message under the name 'Brandon' catches his attention. The last text he sent her reads:

"Hey cuz, I got a question."

That's it. There is no proof of her talking to a plethora of men. Mike is being paranoid for no reason. With the role Kim plays in her job, she doesn't have time to date around. Mike is unaware he is the first man she made time for in almost three years.

Kim returns naked five minutes later and gets underneath the sheets. She turns to look at her phone giving Mike a nice view from behind. His hand can't help but to begin to gentle massage her side. She puts the phone down and cuddles inside Mike's arms.

He rubs her soft booty before slowly working his way up to the top of her back. He then kisses all over her shoulders. Her body responds by rising up and getting ready to ride his dick, cowboy style.

She thrusts herself repeatedly on his pelvis. It starts off slowly at first but she eventually picks up speed. Her moans get louder each time. Mikes eyes roll in the back of his head. He feels the nut slowly rushing to the surface. They start talking *'dirty'* to each other which enhances the experience.

"God damn baby, ride this dick! Ride it!"

Kim has her head thrown all the way back while yelling louder.

"Ooooo Give it to me harder daddy!" Kim's whole body is beginning to shake. Mike throws her onto the bed thrusting between her thighs. This drives Kim's G-spot wild. Mike knows he's a few strokes away from finishing.

After a few minutes of thrusting, His penis begins pulsating. A pleasuring sexual high exerts all over his brain sending Mike over the edge. He lets out one last moan before the exhaustion hits. Kim catches her breath while lying on Mike's chest. He feels her juices all over his private area. She falls asleep with Mike stroking her hair. Her scent makes him consider settling down soon. They awake the following day. Still lying in bed, Kim turns over to Mike.

"Good morning handsome. Hope you enjoyed it."

Choose what Mike does next:

Turn to page 84 if Mike feels the sex was disappointing.

Turn to page 75 if Mike feels the sex was everything he hoped.

Turn to page 85 if Mike asks if she does threesomes.

Mike can't get enough of Kim's sex.

"I have to admit, that was everything I hoped it would be." He says while still exhausted.

Kim smiles while running her finger down his muscular chest. She admires how toned his body is. They eventually get out of bed and go through their morning routine. As they both get dressed, Mike makes a suggestion.

"Let's do something spontaneous. I have an RV that I usually take to the beach every now and then. Would you like to go?"

 "When you said beach you already had me. Let's go." Kim happily answers.

Kim switches into her beach attire. After grabbing a beach towel, they head to Mikes apartment so he can change as well.

Afterwards, they both head to the other side of town where he keeps his RV stored. He swaps his car in place of the RV. They eventually make it to the beach. Mike pulls out a canopy and sets his whole site up. Noon arrives and the sun beams down on them. Kim is playing around in the water. Mike relaxes under the shade of the RV's awning. He notices another attractive woman in the distance. She marvels at the RV's features.

The woman is aware he's with Kim. She walks over and discreetly slides Mike a small piece of paper before leaving. It has her number along with the name 'Diamond' on it. Kim returns to the RV after seeing her.

"Did you know that girl?"

Mike shakes his head no.

Kim responds,

"I swear, these shanks have no shame. I know she saw us together."

Mike has the paper hidden in his fist. He wonders if he should tell Kim about it. They aren't together, so technically he doesn't owe her any loyalty. But at the same time, Kim seems like a real catch. Mike is torn on what he should do.

Make a choice

Choose what Mike does next:

Turn to page 80 if Mike shows Kim the paper.

Turn to page 78 if Mike keeps it a secret.

Mike doesn't owe Kim any loyalty. Why should he tell her about Diamond's number? They are technically just dating right now. If things get more serious he'll give her the exclusive treatment.

Mike blows the situation off as if nothing happened. Kim believes him. In the back of his mind, He wonders about her name. 'Diamond' has to be a nick name. Her body is better than Kim's. Mike definitely plans to sleep with her. Time goes on as Kim and Mike enjoy the beach. They eventually head back to drop the RV off and then back to their own houses.

Later that night, Mike starts to think about how curvy Diamond looked in her two piece bathing suit. He immediately texts her.

"Hey, This Mike from the beach. WYD?"

Diamond texts back a few minutes later.

"Nothing, at work. You should come see me."

At work? It's almost 12 P.M. she must be a nurse of something. All Mike knows is she wants him to come through and kick it with her. He knows how tiring those grave yard shifts can be. Mike gets up ready to meet Diamond where she's at.

"Cool. I'll be there. Where is your job?"

Diamond responds back

"Fantasys, Off Barkley Ave."

Fantasys? Everyone in the city knows that place is a strip club. Suddenly everything makes sense. Kim texts him a few seconds later.

"Hey, I really enjoyed hanging out with you today. I haven't been this excited about someone in a long time. Good night."

Mike knows he has a good girl in Kim on his hands. He wants to do her right. But Mike still wants to experience Diamond at the same time.

Choose what Mike does next:

Turn to page 57 if Mike deletes Diamonds number and focuses on Kim

Turn to page 71 if Mike jumps in his car to have a good time with Diamond.

Mike knows what he has with Kim. He doesn't want to jeopardize it over some big booty broad named Diamond. He gives Kim the paper.

"As you can see, the ladies love Mike. But you the only one I want." He jokes.

Kim is impressed that he revealed her number to him.

"Yeah yeah don't let it go to your head. You not that fine." She jokes back with a smile.

They wrap it up at the beach and head back to Kim's house. She invites Mike to stay one more night. He knows he has to return to his apartment in order to get more clothes to wear. He decides to make the trip.

After dropping the RV and Kim off, Mike decides to head home. While driving, he accidently strikes something that forces his car to a complete stop. He dizzyingly hops out only to notice a strange creature lying on the ground. The monster has no pupils. It wears a tarnished red cap resembling something out of a comic book. Mike watches it rise while yelling in a fit of rage. Suddenly another man wearing a cape arrives. His muscles are chiseled. His suit is alien. His appearance is that of your typical superhero. Mike watches in disbelief.

"What the fuck? Am I on a movie set??" he asks himself.

The superhero has a red lightning bolt symbol on his chest. He gives the creature's jaw a superman style punch. This sends it flying away. The hero flies after the creature, never to be seen again. Mike is in disbelief.

He immediately calls Kim and tries to explain what occurred. She laughs him off before asking how long it will take him to arrive. The next day, Mike takes his story to the media. Nobody believes him. He quits his job and dedicates the rest of his life vowing to find the hero he saw that night.

You've reached a dead end.

Make another choice on page 77

Reality kicks in. Mike is in a millionaire's house. Her wallet is fully exposed. Forget about the phone, Mike wants that credit card! He knows it will completely change his life. He reaches over and flips it open. Mike struggles to find the credit card inside. Kim walks in, silently watching Mike look through her wallet.

"What the fuck do you think you're doing?"

Mike startlingly jumps up. He comes up with the worst excuse ever.

"Nothing, I was looking for my credit card!"

Kim knows he's full of shit. Her wallet is pink. There's no way he could've actually gotten them confused.

"Get the fuck out my house right now!" she furiously demands.

Ashamed, Mike grabs his things and heads out the door.

"And don't even think about coming back to work! You're fired! Trifling ass!" Kim yells out before he makes it to his car.

Looks like Mike got fired on his day off. There's a movie reference in there somewhere……

You've reached a dead end.

Make another choice on page 70

Despite Kim's feelings, Mike believes the sex was trash. As a matter of fact, he was so turned off that he immediately grabs his belongings and heads out the door. Kim is confused.

"Mike, what's going on? Is it something I did?"

"No, it's not you. It's me. I should've never come here. You are my boss. We can't do this."

Kim immediately feels ashamed. She knows he's right. Eventually the weekend passes. Mike returns to work. He notices Kim acting very peculiar. She purposely avoids him at all costs. Mike feels bad about leaving her the way he did. He tries to apologize the next time he sees her. She wasn't hearing any of it. Mike works for the company for another 3 years. He never gets a promotion. Kim has apparently blackballed him. He quits, only to become a trash collector due to the bad economy.

You've reached a dead end.

Make another choice on page 74

"How do you feel about having sex with me...and another woman at the same time?"

Mike asks curiously.

"I'm not really into women like that" She responds.

Mike is disappointed, until she finishes her sentence.

"But I would if you wanted to."

He gets hype. The only thing he can think about was who to bring into the mix. Maybe they can go looking for a girl together. Oh the possibilities.   Both Mike's mind and his hormones race with excitement. But he gives a relaxed response.

"That's what's up!"

Mike and Kim hit the club that night and find a woman they see as attractive. She agrees to sleep with them. For the next three months, they have a threesome with her on a weekly basis. Both Mike and Kim soon begin feeling ill. It isn't the usual sickness that he gets after catching a bug. There is something different about it that worries them both.

They decide to visit a doctor together to get to the bottom it. After a blood test, the doctor informs them that they've both tested positive for HIV. Kim can't handle the news. She overdoses on pills and is found dead by Mike that same night. Her company is left to her surviving relatives who sell it off to one of Black Rose Inc's biggest competitors. Mike doesn't see a dime of that money and declines the offer to keep his position during the acquisition. Saddened by how his life turned out, He takes his RV out of storage permanently and lives off the grid. No one sees or hears from Mike again.

You've reached a dead end.

Make another choice on page 74

The C.E.O. and the office worker

Alternate Ending #2

After having sex with Diamond in the VIP lounge, Mike's brain finally overrides his hormones. He knows there is no future with her and doesn't intend on keeping in contact beyond that night. Once Diamonds shift is over, they have a heart to heart conversation. Mike starts off by walking her to the parking lot. She is fully clothed wearing blue jeans and a red halter top. He decides to ask the obvious question.

"So why did you let me hit for free?"

Diamond looks away. Sadness fills her eyes.

"I just needed my own escape. And you were the only attractive man in there tonight." She replies.

"Escape from what?"

Mike leans against her car stroking her back while she leans in his muscular arms.

"The truth is I hate stripping. But I don't have any other way to support my son."

Thoughts cross Mike's head. He's curious as to why she can't get a job like everyone else. Despite that curiosity, he doesn't ask. He appreciates her vulnerability.

"What's your real name Diamond?" He asks.

"Tiffany." She says.

Mike notices the parking lot has emptied out.

"How were you planning to get home?"

Tiffany continues shamefully look away.

"I was going to catch the bus." She says.

Mike offers to give Tiffany a ride.

"The next one won't be here for another two hours. Let me take you home."

She hesitates at first but decides it's better than sitting on the bench waiting for the next one to arrive. Mike ends up dropping Tiffany off at her apartments. he accepts her offer for a chance to stay the night. Mike forgoes sex to simply hold her.

He awakes the next day feeling Tiffany still sleeping under his arm. He immediately checks his phone and notices a good morning text from Kim. He knows he has to make a choice. There is something about Tiffany's personality that intrigues him. Later that day, he makes his decision. He calls Kim and lets her know his heart belongs to someone else. Although Kim is saddened, she understands.

Mike then convinces Tiffany to quit stripping. In turn she moves in with him and finishes school on his dime. While in between jobs, she contributes with stay at home mom duties. One day, Mike gets off work and finds Tiffany in bed with another man. After an intense interrogation, she reveals that he is in fact an Ex whom she never got over. Mike is on the fence about putting her and her son out on the street. He decides to give her a week to find somewhere else to stay. Tiffany quickly moves in with the Ex. He regrets not choosing Kim. She is now married with a little one on the way.

Return to page 9 and see if you can find your way to alternate ending #1.

The Best Friend

This story has two alternative endings. See if you can find your way past the dead ends to reach them.

Choose Wisely.

Brittany, a flight attendant, currently works for one of the biggest airlines in America. She exits the airport after finishing a shift and heads home to cook for her husband Jason. While driving, She gets a call from her college best friend, Shantelle.

"Hello?" Brittany answers.

"Hey. What you doing?"

"Nothing much, just getting off work. You?"

"Girl, you will not believe what just happened to me today! The bank let me go!" Shantelle passionately responds.

Brittany is saddened by her friend's situation. You see, Shantelle was one of her biggest supporters back in their college years. Brittany's mother died, causing her to fall into a deep depression. Shantelle was there reminding her of the inner strength she has to endure anything. Brittany often credits part of her success to Shantelle.

"What happened?" Brittany asks.

"It's a long story. I'll tell you about it later." Shantelle says in a shaken voice.

"But what am I going to do now? Where will I live?"

Brittany doesn't want to disregard her friend in her time of need. But at the same time, she isn't fond of idea of another woman living with her and her husband. To make things worse, He usually works nights and weekends. This would leave them alone throughout the week. Brittany remembers well how Shantelle barely wore any clothing back in their college years. She doubts anything has changed.

Choose what Brittany does next:

Turn to page 99 if Brittany decides to be a good friend and let's Shantelle stay until she gets on her feet.

Turn to page 96 if Brittany doesn't feel comfortable with the idea of having another woman around her husband.

Nancy knows the damage is done. Brian tries comforting her once Josh leaves.

"Fuck him! Let's finish what we started."

Nancy is enraged.

"GET THE FUCK OUT OF MY HOUSE RIGHT NOW!"

She pushes him out the master bedroom. Brian blows her off and heads out the front door. With him out of the picture, Nancy's highest priority is saving her marriage. She knows it's a long shot but is determined to try. She starts by calling Josh's phone ten times a day. She finds out he still wants to be in Dria's life. They agree to let him keep her on the weekends. Nancy tries sparking up a conversation when he arrives but never gets anywhere. One Friday, Josh comes to pick her up while in a good mood. He agrees to meet up for dinner. Ironically that same day, she throws up in the bathroom.

Proceed to page 237

Brittany can't fathom the idea of her husband messing around on her. She trusts her friend. Eventually, her week long flight ends returning Brittany to her home town. She notices Jason is the happiest she's seen him in a long time. Shantelle is living her best life as well. Things couldn't be more perfect around the house. Why change anything?

Shantelle gets a job as a waitress six months later. She works weekends while she attends college at the same time. Brittany moves on to the administrative side of the airline. Her desk job no longer requires her to travel.

Jason and Shantelle became best friends in Brittany's eyes. They often go out to clubs, bars, theme parks, and anywhere else the city has to offer. They currently have a Disney world trip coming up to celebrate Shantelle's new job. Brittany wants go but is unable to take the day off due to a very important business meeting. She's fine with them vacationing without her. She knows they will never cross the line.....

Dead End

You've reached a dead end.

If you're finished basking in your delusion make another choice on page 122

Brittany isn't a fool. The idea of her husband and best friend alone in her house drives her insane. While she sympathizes with Shantelle's situation, she can't allow her to move in.

"Damn girl, I'll keep you in my prayers."

Shantelle doesn't take the hint. She flat out asks,

"Do you think it would be alright if I stayed with you? I just need a little time to get my life together."

Brittany feels like a deer trapped in headlines. She doesn't want to hurt her friend's feelings. But at the same time she doesn't want to invite unnecessary drama in her house. She decides to tell her the truth.

"I'm sorry but I'm married. That would leave my husband home alone with another woman. I can't."

Shantelle is hurt by Brittany's words.

"Girl! Nobody want's your husband! But it's cool. I'll figure something out."

Brittany feels guilty for turning her back on Shantelle. But it doesn't matter. The damage is already done.

Brittany learns about karma the hard way. Brittany and Shantelle cease communication. A year later, she gets laid off due to the airline going out of business. Jason is now paralyzed from a work injury involving the top step of a ladder a month prior. He now depends on Brittany to live. She knows everything is about to come crashing down on them.

Jason watches the news when Brittany walks through the door. She is still visibly upset yet unsure how to tell Jason. Before she could get a word out, he turns and asks:

"Hey, is this your friend on T.V.?"

Brittany can't believe her eyes. Shantelle stands next to a news reporter in front of a well-known restaurant. Getting fired from the bank motivated her to open up a franchise. She just so happened to have met a guy who also lost his job. He had just enough money left in savings to invest. Their business took off as soon as they opened the doors.

Shantelle is now well on her way to becoming a millionaire. Brittany regrets not helping her friend that day. She calls Shantelle to apologize and congratulate her on her success that same night. Shantelle surprising answers, revealing she isn't holding any grudges over the situation. The conversation is cut short due to her busy work schedule. Shantelle and the man eventually get married and open up 20 more locations within a 5 year span.

Together, they make over 50 million dollars. Brittany and Jason's living situation gets worse. Finances force them to downgrade to a trailer park. After an employee quits, Shantelle calls Brittany to offer her a job. Brittany now works as a hostess.

You've reached a dead end.

Make another choice on page 92

Brittany knows she can't allow Shantelle to be homeless.

"Girl you know you are welcomed inside my castle anytime. You can stay as long as you need." She offers.

Shantelle chokes up before declining.

"Nah, I don't wanna be a burden. I've been researching some shelters in the ar-"

Brittany interrupts her mid-sentence.

"A shelter? When we got a big 2 story house available? I won't take no for an answer. Bring yo' butt over here and unpack your bags."

Shantelle finally gives in. You can hear the optimism in her voice.

"Well if you insist."

"I'll have dinner ready by the time you get here." The call ends.

Brittany arrives at her home moments later. She walks through the door and see's Jason getting dressed for work. He's a manager at a warehouse overseeing the graveyard shift.

"Hey honey. How was your day?" Brittany asks.

"Can't complain." He responds.

Jason then reclines in his living room chair. He has a thirty minute window to relax before its time for work. Brittany decides to lay the news on him.

"So Shantelle lost her job today."

"Damn, that's messed up."

Jason nonchalantly says.

You can tell he really doesn't care. Brittany, always telling her husband everything, continues the conversation.

"Yeah, apparently the bank was tripping and let her go. I told her she could stay with us until she gets on her feet."

Jason gets irritated.

"Don't you think that's something we should've discussed first? You can't make big decisions like that without me!"

Brittany defends her friend.

"You know Shantelle has nowhere to go!"

In that moment, the doorbell rings. Brittany blows the petty argument off and let's Shantelle inside. She enters with two suitcases and a bag full of toiletries. She wears a short revealing sundress. Jason's neck almost breaks at the sight of her. Brittany shows Shantelle to the guest room.

Choose what Brittany does next:

Turn to page 105 if Brittany tells Shantelle to dress appropriately while around her husband.

Turn to page 109 if Brittany let's Shantelle wear whatever makes her happy.

As the old saying goes, *'Mama ain't raise no fool!'* The sight of Shantelle and Jason watching TV in the dark is too much for Brittany to bear.

"What the fuck is going on here?" she yells, causing the passengers on the plane to gasp.

Patricia tries to calm Brittany down.

"Would you please lower your voice?"

Brittany ignores her and continues her wrath on Shantelle.

"I SAID WHAT THE FUCK IS GOING ON?"

"Nothing is going on! And why are you cussing at me?" Shantelle responds.

This only pisses Brittany off even more.

"You are home alone snuggled up with my husband in the dark! Don't try to play me like I'm a fucking idiot Shantelle!"

The passengers are all appalled at her foul language. Patricia tries to distract them by starting the food cart down the aisle.

Jason quickly snatches the phone from Shantelle. He puts himself on the screen.

"Baby…Baby, calm down! It's not what it looks like!" He pleads.

"What do you mean it's not what it looks like? You conveniently took the week off knowing I won't be home until Friday!"

"Dammit woman! We're just lying under a damn blanket. You act like we fucking or someth-"

The call suddenly drops. Shantelle got tired of hearing Brittany's mouth and ended it for Jason. Brittany tries calling back. The video call is never answered. Without thinking, she grabs a pen out of her purse and races to the pilot's cockpit. She bangs on the door until he finally answers.

Brittany then yells while holding the pen up to his throat,

"Turn this got damn plane around right now!"

This causes all the passengers to panic. The co-pilot immediately jumps out of his seat and subdues Brittany by grabbing her other arm. She is immediately brought down. Once on the ground, she yells:

"GET THE FUCK OFF ME AND TURN THIS DAMN PLANE AROUND!"

Brittany gets restrained in a chair. Due to the circumstances, the plane is forced to head back to its original airport. After landing, Brittany is handed over to the authorities. She gets a 12 years prison sentence for making a terroristic threat mid-flight. Jason divorces Brittany shortly afterwards.

You've reached a dead end.

Make another choice on page 108

Brittany unloads Shantelle's luggage in the guest room. While unpacking, She sets some ground rules.

"Don't take this the wrong way, but I'd prefer you not wear anything too revealing around my husband."

Shantelle acknowledges her friends request.

"Okay."

The next day Brittany awakes at the crack of dawn to begin her shift. After getting dressed, she heads to work. While there, she is surprised to learn about an overseas flight she's been assigned to. She won't be back for another five days. She calls and informs her husband. Luckily the flight has Wi-Fi, so Brittany will be able to video chat with him whenever she wants.

First day on the flight, Brittany and her coworker Patricia take sleeping shifts. Brittany video chats with Jason before the sun sets back at home. Their conversation is nothing out of the ordinary. Jason is preparing for another shift at the warehouse. Shantelle washes dishes in the background.

"Hey baby, Just wanted to see how you were holding up."

Jason smiles.

"Everything is good. Shantelle just got done throwing down in the kitchen! Why didn't you tell me she could cook?"

Brittany laughs. Shantelle shouts from the back,

"I hope you don't mind! We were both starving!"

"Girl please! I appreciate you for stepping in!"

Jason's demeanor reveals he is in a hurry.

"Well baby I gotta go. Work is calling my name. I'll talk to you tomorrow!"

"BYE FRIEND!" Shantelle yells in a friendly tone.

Brittany ends the call and returns to sleep.

The next day, after completing a long shift, she alternates with Patricia. Brittany then checks her watch to verify its sunset back at home. She calls her husband using the video chat app on her phone once again. This time, something seems a little off.

"Hey baby! How's your day?" she asks.

She sees Jason relaxing on the couch while watching a movie. He immediately hits the pause button.

"Hey big head. It was alright. I got to finally get some rest. Work has been hella stressful lately."

Brittany notices her husband is wrapped their favorite cuddling blanket. This is breaking routine, being that he usually gets ready for work around this time.

"You don't have to work tonight?" she asks.

Jason quickly answers.

"Well baby, I've been working really hard for the past two weeks. I've decided to take some time for me."

An uneasy feeling hits Brittany's stomach. Despite her intuition telling her otherwise, she chooses to have faith in her husband. She doesn't see him betraying her after 9 years of marriage.

"Good for you." She responds.

Suddenly the phone shifts.

"HEEEEEEY GIRLL!" Shantelle says in an excited tone.

She is seen sitting on the other side of the couch. Although the phone remains above her waist, Brittany gets a glimpse of Shantelle's blanket while the phone shifts. It is the same as Jason! Brittany is too confused.

Choose what Brittany does next:

Turn to page 120 if Brittany doesn't think anything of it.

Turn to page 117 if Brittany says "Don't hey girl me! Why you snuggled up in the dark with my husband?"

Turn to page 102 if Brittany high jacks the plane and forces the pilot to turn around.

Brittany isn't concerned about Shantelle's clothing. She knows this is her friends time of need right now. What isn't needed is a man trying to dictate what she wears.

Shortly after showing Shantelle to her room, Brittany gets in the shower and prepares for bed. Jason has since gone off to work. Brittany awakens the next day. She is scheduled to work two flights at two hours each. This leaves her enough time to be back for dinner. Her brother Derek briefly calls, mentioning that he'd stop by sometime during the week to fix a leaking pipe in her ceiling.

One of the flights gets canceled due to an engine malfunction. Brittany is allowed to return home early. Once there, she walks through the door and into chaos. Shantelle and Jason are seen arguing with Derek. The accusation he makes is startling.

"I CAUGHT YOU TWO HAVING SEX!" Derek yells at Jason.

Jason turns to Brittany then yells,

"DON'T LISTEN TO HIM! HE'S LYING!" He pleads with her.

Tears form in her eyes.

"What?" is all she can muster.

"ITS NOT TRUE BRITTANY!" Shantelle adds.

Derek looks Brittany in the eyes,

"WOULD I LIE TO YOU OVER SOMETHING LIKE THIS?"

The sincerity on Derek's face convinces Brittany that he speaks the truth. In a jealous rage, she grabs a butcher knife. She then stares down the woman who betrayed her trust. Her demeanor shows a psychotic side has surfaced. She is prepared to end Shantelle's life if the accusations are true. She asks in a very calm yet disappointed voice.

"Is this true?"

Jason speaks for Shantelle.

"WHAT THE FUCK BRITTANY, NO! ARE YOU GOING TO BELIEVE HIM OVER YOUR OWN HUSBAND?"

Shantelle refuses to look Brittany in the eyes. Brittany continues to give her a death stare.

"BITCH YOU DID FUCK MY HUSBAND! I'M GOING TO KILL YOU!"

Just like that, she races towards Shantelle with the knife. Jason tries holding her back and gets stabbed in the process. The knife punctures his heart, killing him. Brittany becomes distraught over seeing her husband lifeless on the floor like that. Derek and Shantelle can't believe what they just witnessed.

Brittany drops to her knees crying in despair. Derek attempts to suppress Jason's wound, unaware that he is already gone. Brittany feels powerless while watching. The sight of her deceased husband overwhelms her.

Without thinking, she slashes her own throat. Her body poetically drops next to his. Derek sobs while catching her head in his lap. He tries applying pressure on the wound but to no avail. During her last moments of life, she stares into her husband's lifeless eyes. The blood slowly chokes her to death. Instead of helping, Shantelle bolts to her car. She drives off and is never seen again.

It's still not clear whether Jason actually cheated on her or not.

You've reached a dead end.

Make another choice on page 101

Brittany returns home later that week. She figures Jason and Shantelle are sleeping together behind her back but has no evidence to prove it. It matters not. She has her own little side piece to play with at this point. Brittany returns home and showers. She then eats Shantelle's cooking and is surprised at how delicious it is. Jason acts happy to see her but gets a dry response.

"Is Brittany okay?" Shantelle questions Jason.

He just shrugs, writing it off as jet lag. They then proceed to binge watch Netflix on the living room couch. Expecting Brittany to join, they are surprised to see her turn into the master bedroom. She secretly sends Kevin a bunch of nude photos to play with his mind. Around 9:00 P.M. Jason knocks on the door and asks if Brittany is interested in going to the club with him. She declines.

"I'm way too exhausted for that."

Brittany knows she's lying. The club would actually be a good stress reliever. But she's not feeling the idea of going anywhere with her husband. He disgusts her right now. Every thought is accompanied by visuals of him having sex with Shantelle in their bed. Kevin on the other hand seems to be a ray of light in the darkness. The dick pics he sent have her whole body yearning for more.

"You sure you don't wanna go out? They say Trey Songz is going to perform." Jason asks once more in hopes Brittany will change her mind.

He knows Trey Songz is Brittany's celebrity crush. But she isn't going for it and declines again. Shantelle decides to take him up on his offer.

"I'll go with you." She says.

Brittany swings the door open, flabbergasted at Shantelle's boldness.

"Excuse me?"

Brittany isn't even mad about the idea of them on a date together. It's clear they're cheating. She's more appalled at the blatant disrespect under her roof. Shantelle tries to keep the peace.

"I hope you don't mind. After last week I could use a drink and some Trey Songz in my life."

It was then Brittany got a text message from Kevin. It read:

"Can you get out tonight?"

If she could smile in that moment she would. She calms down in order to get rid of her husband.

"Do what ya'll want. I'm going to bed." Brittany says while shutting the door softly.

Jason and Shantelle confusingly look at each other.

"She mad about something. Let's give her some time to cool off." He tells Shantelle. She nods in agreement. Minutes later, Brittany hears Jason's truck pull out the driveway. She looks out the window to verify they left.

Brittany calls Kevin to let him know she's free.

"Hey. I don't have a lot of time before he gets back. Wanna get a room?"

Kevin doesn't hesitate to say yes. They pick a nearby budget motel to meet at. Brittany steps out in her sleeping clothes. She meets Kevin at the room they were assigned. Brittany's husband calls out of nowhere. He and Shantelle decided to hold off on the club until Brittany was in a better mood. They returned home only to notice she was gone. Brittany has 15 missed back to back calls from Jason. He also sends an angry text message:

"Where are you? And why aren't you answering my calls?"

Choose what Brittany does next:

Turn to page 126 if Brittany ignores his cheating ass and decides to spend the night with Kevin at the motel.

Turn to page 139 if Brittany tells Kevin she can't do this and returns home to her husband.

Brittany snaps at Shantelle.

"Don't hey girl me! Why you snuggled up with my husband in the dark??"

This annoys all passengers on the airline. It's dark outside and they're all trying to sleep after all.

"What are you talking about?? We're not even on the same side of the couch...." Shantelle confusingly asks.

She then aims the phone down, revealing her uncovered legs. This has Brittany baffled.

"I'm not using a blanket!" Shantelle reponds.

Brittany is sure of what she saw. She's convinced Shantelle is pulling a fast one on her. But without any concrete evidence, there's nothing she can do. Brittany decides to let it go.

"Girl I apologize. This flight must've taken more of a toll on me than I thought."

Shantelle sympathizes.

"Now you know I wouldn't betray you of all people like that! We've been best friends since college!"
Jason grabs the phone and rushes Brittany off.

"Now that we're past that, we about to turn this Denzel movie back on. Plus I know you got sleep to catch. Good night baby."

Before Brittany could respond the video ends. She knows Denzel Washington is her husband's idol. They usually watch all his movies together. She can't help but to feel a little jealous. She eventually falls asleep in her seat.

Day 3 goes by. The time to call her husband draws near. Brittany feels terrible about the way she reacted to Shantelle and decides to make it up to her with their next conversation. The plane lands overseas at an airport to unload the passengers. Brittany has a four hour break window. She decides to video chat with her husband an hour early. She calls only to get a pitch black screen when he answers.

"Baby, are you there?" She asks.

Brittany figures Jason must have accidentally picked it up. While she does hear voices in the background, she gets no response. Brittany decides to listen carefully. She hears Shantelle softly moaning.

"Mmmmm.....oooooo! That feels good! Thank you for this..."

"Now wait a minute! What's going on?? Hello??" Brittany asks in agitation.

Still no answer. The sexual talk continues.

"I definitely needed that..." Shantelle says in a sexual voice.

Ironically, standing before her is a very attractive business man who can't keep his eyes off Brittany.

Choose what Brittany does next:

Turn to page 123 if Brittany decides two can play at that game.

Turn to page 136 if Brittany remains faithful to her husband and plans to handle the situation when she returns.

Brittany doesn't look too deep into the situation. Shantelle is probably cold. Her husband is just being a gentleman like he usually is. Brittany figures they both love her enough not to cross that line.

"Hey girl! How are you enjoying the house so far?" She asks.

Shantelle's body moves in an up and down motion on the couch. But why is she doing that underneath some blankets? Once again, Brittany doesn't look too deep into it. Shantelle continues the conversation.

"I absolutely adore your kitchen! You know how much I love to cook! You got all the right appliances!"

Suddenly it hits Brittany.

"You wanted to open a restaurant one day didn't you?"

"If God says the same it.....will happen." Shantelle struggles to say.

Brittany's is curious as to why Shantelle's eyes keep closing. She also hears a very faint but constant patting movement in the background. She can't tell what it is just yet. But the sound is similar to a pair of jeans being tugged back and forth. There are too many red flags to ignore. Brittany decides to give her a chance to explain.

"Why are you moving around like that? Are you exercising or something?" She asks.

Shantelle ceases her constant back and forth movement. Brittany also hears a voice faintly in the background. The person is trying their best to keep a whispering tone. She can only make out a few words out of their sentence.

"Tell her --- gotta --…" The voice says.

Shante has small talk with Brittany,

"Yes, I was doing some leg squats in between commercials. You know we gotta stay ready to be summer time fine!"

"I hear that." Brittany adds.

"We'll let me get back to this exercising. I'll talk to you later girl!"

"Wait, let me speak to Jason!"

But it was too late. The video call ends abruptly. Why was Shantelle in such a rush to get off the phone? Why didn't Jason tell her good night? Brittany is in need of answers immediately. She finally asks herself the obvious question.

"Are they sneaking around behind my back?"

Choose what Brittany does next:

Turn to page 153 if Brittany is ready to accept the obvious.

Turn to page 94 if Brittany wants to ride this delusional roller coaster just a little bit longer.

It's pretty clear in Brittany's mind that she's being played for a fool. Why else is Shantelle moaning? Brittany is furious at herself for allowing this conniving person inside her castle. But revenge is a dish best served cold. Both Jason and Shantelle are in for a real treat.

Brittany feels the attractive man undressing her with his eyes. She plans to use him as a pawn to get back at her husband. Soon he walks up to her.

"Excuse me miss. I'll give you two options. You can hear something real, or you can get a pick up line. Which will it be?" He says.

Brittany does all the classic things to reel him in. She smiles while never breaking eye contact and slides her wedding ring down into her purse. All of her nonverbal signals fire off how much she likes him.

"Something real." She says in a shy tone.

"You sure you don't want the pickup line? I got a really good one!" Kevin jokes.

Brittany is intrigued at how smooth he is.

"Okay, the pickup line."

Kevin lets off his nice smile while going for the punch line.

"I was actually going to get something to eat. I was wondering if you would hold this..."

Kevin extends his hand. That was so smooth that Brittany can help but hold it. She flirts while smiling from ear to ear. They begin walking to the nearest sandwich shop from within the airport.

Author's note: Yes, this has worked many times back in my college days.

Brittany and Kevin find themselves eating at a nearby deli shop. So far she is really feeling his swag. Throughout their conversation she finds herself laughing at his corny jokes. Brittany's break soon comes to an end. Kevin, as it turns out, is set to board that same flight.

Brittany tells him about her marriage.

"We are going through some problems." She adds. Kevin doesn't mind being the 'other guy' for the time being if that's what she wants. Brittany leaves him with her number before returning to the plane. She promises to text him as soon as she gets home.

Just like that, Brittany has a side piece.

Choose wisely:

Turn to page 113 if Brittany is justified in having a side piece.

Turn to page 129 if Brittany is seeking revenge prematurely. It's still possible her husband isn't cheating.

"He has some nerve!" Brittany contemplates while turning her phone off. After cutting the video feed countless times now he wants to be upset? Brittany harbors no guilt at all. Now Jason gets to experience how frustrating that feeling truly is. Most men can't handle what they dish out. He's no exception.

Kevin jumps in the shower. Brittany undresses and quickly turns the lights off. Lying in bed gives her a chance to contemplate what went wrong in her marriage. She thinks about the vow she made to her husband. Despite that, here she is ready to give another man her body. What does that make her? She doesn't know the answer to that. All she knows is her vagina is throbbing and screaming Kevin's name. She can't resist fingering herself to mitigate her hormones.

Kevin gets out the shower rock hard. He's ready to give Brittany the sexual experience of a life time. Kevin gets on top of Brittany and begins to passionately suck her nipples. She's turned on even more when he flips her body over and has a soft yet firm hold of each breast. He then thrusts his penis inside her throbbing vagina. Five minutes later Brittany is ready to cum. She hasn't had good sex like this in years.

Kevin then cocks one of her legs in the air while lightly choking her. He continues going deeper inside Brittany. His eyes roll to the top of his eyelids while he yells a bunch of nasty things to her.

"Got damn Brittany! This pussy so fuckin' good. This shit is sooo good."

Brittany talks dirty right back. She can feel the sexual climax rising up to the top of her brain.

"OOOO YESS DADDY! FUCK ME! FUCK ME GOOD! YOU GOT SOME GOOD ASS DICK! FUCK ME!" She yells back.

Both Kevin and Brittany's body shiver until they cum. Afterwards, Kevin lies on top of Brittany out of exhaustion.

"You got that good for real!" he jokes while trying to catch his breath.

As flattered as Brittany is, she immediately feels like shit. The sexual high is gone, leaving the reality that she committed an unforgivable act to sinks in. It doesn't matter what Jason did at that point. Revenge sex proves she is no better than him.

Brittany and Kevin exchange their good byes the next day. She heads home to an angry husband and lies claiming she went to blow off steam at her father's house. Jason, wanting to put this behind them, believes her and lets it go. Life continues. Four weeks later, Brittany starts feeling sick in her stomach.

Reality hits home when she takes a pregnancy test that comes back positive. She and Jason have been on rocky terms. Because of that they haven't had sex in over two months. She was sleeping with Kevin the whole time.

Choose what Brittany does next:

Turn to page 130 If she tells Jason she's pregnant with another man's baby.

Turn to page 144 if she takes that secret to the grave.

Authors Note: I was curious to see where your mind was. Morally you are right. Seeking revenge at this stage is a bit premature. Jason and Shantelle look pretty guilty, but Brittany has no physical evidence to prove it. While I would agree in real life, this is Secrecy and Deceit. Hurry on back to page 125 because things are about to get crazy!

Go to page 113 to keep the story going.

Brittany decides to do the right thing and tell Jason the truth. Seeking revenge put her in this situation. Now she has to own up to her mistakes. Shantelle continues sleeping upstairs in the guest room. Jason lies on his favorite couch spot watching sports. Brittany tells him everything.

Jason's facial expression reveals his disappointment in Brittany. She gets defensive and points out all the times he cheated first. Jason simply responds,

"I never cheated on you! Not one fucking time!"

And just like that, Jason storms out the house. He drives off to an unknown destination.

You're on the right track.

Proceed to page 131

The Best Friend

Alternate Ending #1

Shantelle storms down the stairs seconds after Jason left. She looks Brittany dead in the eyes and asks,

"Is it true?"

"Let's not pretend ya'll wasn't in here fucking when I was gone. I heard you moaning over the phone talkin' bout *THANK YOU FOR THIS!* How could you?" Brittany responds, releasing the built up anger she had since this all started.

"Are you referring to the time I tripped at the gym?" Shantelle snaps back.

"My leg landed on some weights and it hurt like hell. Jason noticed how I limbed though the door and was using a mechanical massager to suppress the pain!"

Shantelle's explanation makes Brittany feel even worse than she already did. Everything Shantelle says adds up. But still, Brittany isn't ready to give up the accusations just yet.

"But the sharing covers while watching a movie? Cooking for him? Going out to the club together...."

"We NEVER shared a cover! I sat on the other side of the couch out of respect for your marriage. I even showed you my legs so you could see for yourself!" Shantelle cuts Brittany off.

Brittany drops her head in shame. She knows she messed up big time. Her insecurities caused her to do the unthinkable. Shantelle and Jason's affair was something that only existed inside of her imagination.

"And truth be told I was I cooking for myself! You know that's my passion!" Shantelle continues.

"He liked the smell and wanted a plate, so I made him one!"

Brittany continues to listen.

"As for the club, I'm the reason we turned around soon as we got half way there! I didn't feel right being alone with Jason!" Shantelle says before storming back into the guest room. She immediately packs her bags.

Brittany stands just outside the hallway.

"Wait! Don't leave?" she pleads.

Shantelle has had enough of being caught in the middle of their marriage.

"You really fucked up this time. And I can't help you out of this one!" she responds.

Shantelle quickly carries her suitcases and toiletry bags downstairs. She heads outside towards her car. Brittany powerlessly watches her walk out the door. Before closing it, Shantelle leaves Brittany with something to think about:

"You are my best friend and I still love you, but you got some serious soul searching to do."

Now Brittany is alone in her house with a child on the way. She heads into her bed and cries herself to sleep. Jason returns home later that night. He sits in deep thought on the couch. Finding out your wife is pregnant with another man's seed isn't an easy thing to deal with.

After hours of countless apologies from Brittany, he agrees to attend a marriage counseling session. It was there he was able to see things through his wife's point of view. He understands how his actions were interpreted as cheating. Despite that understanding, Jason knows he's not emotionally capable of remaining in that marriage. He files for divorce and moves out shortly after.

Surprisingly both Jason and Shantelle show up at the hospital when Brittany gives birth to a baby girl. Kevin denies being the father and is nowhere to be found. Shantelle and Brittany's relationship never truly recovers from that incident. They eventually fall out altogether. Brittany sends Jason a text every once in a while. His slow responses reveal he hasn't forgiven her for the betrayal. Despite that, Brittany continues to be a good mother and hopes he will one day. For now she gives him all the space he needs.

Return to page 108 and see if you can find your way to alternate ending #2.

Nancy takes her secret to the grave. They continue on with their marriage as two years pass. Josh takes his daughter Dria to the doctor for her annual shots. After taking one good look, the doctor suggests a DNA test. Josh is offended. He knows his wife would never cheat. The doctor's persistence convinces him to do it anyway. The results are scheduled to arrive in the mail in a few days. After leaving, he jumps on the phone with Nancy.

"Hey baby. We just left the doctor's office. He suggested I take a DNA test for some weird reason." He says. His tone suggests he's not worried.

Nancy turns into a nervous wreck on the inside. This could expose her. Maybe it's time to confess...

Choose what Nancy does next:

Turn to page 203 if Nancy tells Josh the truth.

Turn to page 13 if Nancy continues the charade.

Brittany blows the business man off. The temptation to cheat calls her name but she isn't that type of girl. She avoids eye contact and heads back to her terminal. The man walks over to her and introduces himself. Brittany walks off in response.

"Well fuck you too bitch! You ugly anyway!" he yells before walking away.

Brittany is offended by his words. She decides to blow it off and heads into a restroom minutes before her flight. Inside, a strange woman wearing gypsy clothing is seen staring in the mirror. Brittany heads into a stall and does her private business. She then proceeds to the sink to wash her hands. When attempting to leave, the gypsy pulls her hand.

"Um, excuse me????" Brittany yanks her hand back.

"I'm sorry ma'am, but I'm down on my luck. Do you have some money to spare?" she asks.

Brittany knows she has forty dollars in her pocket. But she isn't feeling very charitable.

"I'm sorry but I don't."

Brittany proceeds to walk off with goose bumps forming all over her.

"Why did you lie?"

"What?" Brittany says confusingly.

"You have 40 dollars located in the back corner pocket of your purse. Why did you lie?"

At this point Brittany is ready scream for help. Exactly how did the gypsy get it right? She mentioned the exact amount currently in Brittany's purse. What's even stranger is no one has entered the bathroom since she walked in. The once noisy airport is now dead silent.

"I didn't lie! That money is reserved for something else! Now fuck off!" She snaps before storming out of the bathroom.

Brittany steps out to an empty airport. It's clear as day outside. The planes sit on the runway with no people around. Everyone vanished without a trace. The gypsy put a spell on Brittany as soon as she walked through the door. Brittany turns to see her one last time, standing at the entrance.

"What did you do to me???" she asks hysterically.

"People like you are all the same. All the privilege in the world! Yet you do nothing to help those with less!" The gypsy says.

"I CAN'T SAVE THE FUCKING WORLD! IM NOT RICH! WHAT DO YOU WANT ME TO DO?" Brittany angrily responds.

The gypsy shakes her head.

"Good luck getting out of here." She taunts before dissipating into dust. This leaves Brittany alone with endless questions. She roams the airport seeking an exit for what feels like an eternity. She never finds one.

You've reached a dead end.

Make another choice on page 119

Brittany has a change of heart. The stage has been set to extract revenge but she no longer wants it. She turns to Kevin.

"I'm sorry, I can't do this." She says.

He looks confused. Brittany then races back to her car. She attempts to drives off before being blocked in by Kevin. If she hits reverse she risks running him over.

Choose what Brittany does next:

Turn to page 143 if she runs Kevin over.

Turn to page 140 if she gets out the car and hears him out.

Brittany is no killer. It's not in her heart to run anyone over. She revvs the engine up hoping Kevin would get the message. He doesn't move an inch.

"CAN YOU GET OUT AND TALK TO ME?" He yells at her.

She turns the car off and steps out. Kevin walks over to Brittany and tries embracing her. She pulls back.

"Brittany, are you okay?" he asks.

"I have to apologies for bringing you into this. I've realized I don't want to cheat on my husband." She responds. Kevin doesn't believe her.

"If you felt that way, we wouldn't be standing here now." He answers.

"After tonight if you never want to speak again that's fine. But we're here now. The room is paid for. Let's enjoy ourselves while the opportunity is here."

Man Kevin sure does have a way with words. Brittany's horniness takes over. She decides to finish what she started. She will deal with the consequences tomorrow, or so she thought. Jason knows exactly where she is thanks to a tracker he put on her phone. He's not happy about it. A loud bang is heard on the door. His voice yells from the other side.

"BRITTANY I KNOW YOU IN THERE! OPEN UP! WHO ELSE IN THERE WITH YOU?"

Brittany's heart sinks to the floor. She sees Jason and Shantelle standing outside through the blinds. She can tell Jason's out for blood. If he sees Kevin things will get ugly. Kevin reaches in his back pocket and pulls out a gun. Jason manages to breaks the door down and is shot dead. Shantelle gets shot in the back running for her life and plays dead. Brittany gasps out of fear as Kevin turns the gun on her. Instead of firing, he holds her hostage.

"GET IN THE FUCKING CAR NOW!"

Kevin forces Brittany into his trunk. He starts the car and heads towards Mexico. Brittany is never seen or heard from again. Shantelle makes a full recovery in the hospital months later and returns to society. One day while watching the news, she notices a particular story speaking about a man running an illegal prostitution ring in Guadalajara. She is shocked to see Kevin's picture up on the screen.

You've reached a dead end.

Choose a different path on page 116

Make a difference choice on the previous page 139

Brittany decides she's had enough. She hits the gas and runs Kevin over without a second thought. He flies lifelessly onto the concrete. Brittany sees him in the rearview and doesn't know if he survived the impact or not. She desperately races out of the area and returns home.

Needless to say Brittany awakens the next day and hears about a dead body found at the motel. Deep regret radiates in her mind. She becomes a recluse soon after. Jason is aware something is different about his wife but can't get her to open up to him. Kevin's sister seeks revenge after getting the call about his death. She reviews the motels camera footage and finds out who killed him. Brittany's license plate number is seen clear as day. She finds Brittany and ties her up in a garage before starting the car. It doesn't take long for the carbon monoxide to enter Brittany's lungs.

You've reached a dead end.

Choose a different path on page 116

Make a difference choice on the previous page 139

Brittany's terrified to tell her husband the truth. Her marriage will surely be over once he finds out. Brittany figures it's better to take the secret to the grave. She doesn't hide the pregnancy and lies about her conception date. Jason couldn't be more excited.

During her pregnancy, Jason becomes a new man. Shantelle gets put out so he can change the guest room into a nursery. They stock up on baby clothes afterwards. This is the marriage Brittany always wanted. She wishes they would've had a child sooner.

Jason's parents get heavily involved in planning the baby shower. This is their first grandchild after all. Guilt plagues Brittany deep down. As the date draws near, she has a change of heart and wants to tell Jason the truth. Why you ask? Well you see, Jason is a black man while Kevin is white. Once the baby is born, it's going to be obvious it's not his. She'd rather spare him the embarrassment in front of their families beforehand.

One week before delivery, Brittany drops the bomb on him.

Proceed

Proceed to page 150 to see the damage you caused.

Brittany decides to be a good sport. She allows Shantelle to tag along in hopes that she will find another man to give her attention to. They jump in the car and arrive at *The Oak Lounge* twenty minutes later. Once inside, Brittany secures a reserved table for everyone.

Jason spends most of the time cracking jokes with Shantelle. Brittany sits next to him feeling more like a fifth wheel than a wife. Shantelle notices her silence and quickly asks,

"Brittany you sure are quiet. Are you okay?"

Quiet? Shantelle is flirting with Brittany's husband in her face. Is she's supposed to be okay? Brittany completely ignores Shantelle and cuts to the chase with Jason.

"Are you fucking her?"

Jason is taken aback by the question.

"What made you ask something like that?" He asks.

Shantelle places her face in her palms out of embarrassment.

"Don't dance around the question Jason. We're in a club full of single men, yet this bitch would rather sit here flirting with you! The writing is on the fucking wall!"

Brittany doesn't break eye contact with Jason. She wants an answer right now. She is not prepared for what comes out of his mouth next. Shantelle and Brittany are both shocked at the same time.

"I want a divorce."

Choose what Brittany does next:

Turn to page 157 If Brittany saw this coming and wants out herself.

Turn to page 159 if Brittany can't believe what she just heard.

Shantelle got Brittany ALL THE WAY FUCKED UP. Brittany knows she looks good. So why is she feeling so neglected her husband? This causes her reach a boiling point.

"GET THE FUCK OUT OF MY HOUSE!" She yells at Shantelle.

Shantelle remembers Brittany fighting a lot back in their college years. She cowers behind Jason as he tries to mitigate the situation.

"Brittany would you calm down?" he asks.

Brittany quickly kicks her heels off and takes out her earrings. She then tries connecting a punch to Shantelle's jaw only to be restrained by her husband. He throws her to the ground before pressing down on her neck with his knee. It snaps, paralyzing Brittany.

Jason is horrified at the sight of her limp body. The police are called and he gets charged with attempted murder of the first degree. Brittany is forced to live the rest of her life in a nursing home as a paraplegic. She has to relearn how to do everything all over again. Jason is sent to prison for twenty years for his crimes. He gives

Shantelle access to his banking information to pay his lawyers off. She transfers the money to her personal account instead and takes off to another state. Her number changes giving him no way to contact her.

You've reached a dead end.

Make another choice on page 156

"What you do mean it's not mine????" Jason yells in anger. Brittany's voice chokes up.

"I lied about where I stayed that night. I actually got a room with another man. It's a strong chance that he is the father."

Jason can't believe what he's hearing. Not only did his wife step out on him, but she brought a child into their marriage. Five minutes of awkward silence follows. Jason stares into his phone the whole time. Brittany hopes an apology will soften the blow.

"I know you are very angry with me. Words cannot express how sorry I am...Is there anything you want to say?"

Jason still says nothing. He retrieves an envelope from his nightstand in the master bedroom and throws it at Brittany. She opens it, revealing cruise tickets inside a card.

"This was going to be my gift to you after our son arrives. Or should I say your son..."

Tears flow out of Brittany's eyes once she reads it. It simply says,

"I'm sorry I've been a terrible husband to you. These are tickets for a week long cruise to Hawaii. I figured we could use a getaway next year.

–Jason"

He originally looked forward to Brittany's reaction. She buries her face in her palms while balling tears out.

"I'm so sorry!!"

She says the one thing NO MAN wants to hear in a situation like this.

"He may be the sperm donor but you can be th-"

This sends Kevin into a rage.

"SAVE IT! YOU ENDED THE MARRIAGE THE MINUTE YOU GOT IN THE CAR TO GO SEE THAT FOOL! I WANT A DIVORCE!"

Jason heads into their master bedroom closet and begins packing his luggage. Brittany sits on the bed powerless to do anything. Before leaving, Jason calmly says,

"I'll still take you to the hospital once your water breaks. But after the kid is born, we are DONE."

Jason then leaves to stay at a friend's house. He keeps his word and rushes Brittany to the hospital when the time comes. The baby comes out a light complexion. A DNA test further confirms Brittany's worst fear. Jason's not the father. He moves on and dates another woman he meets at work. Kevin denies the child until DNA proves he is the father. Kevin quits his job in order to avoid paying child support. Brittany is hated throughout her family for her betrayal. She's also forced to work three jobs to sustain her new life.

You've reached a dead end.

Choose a different path on page 128

Brittany is tired of living in denial. She's ready to accept her husband and best friend are sneaking around behind her back. Every video chat with Jason is cut short for the remainder of the flight. He's always too busy to talk. The flight ends a week later. She returns to her home town without telling Jason hoping to catch them in the act. Brittany walks through the door. Jason is seen on the couch watching sports center.

Shantelle is frying Jason's favorite food, pork chops, in the kitchen. Brittany made them plenty of times for him early on in the marriage. But that's still not enough evidence to put them on blast. Brittany needs more. Jason turns to his wife and speaks,

"Hey! I didn't know you would be back so soon."

Shantelle also greets her friend.

"Hey best friend! How was work?"

Brittany's blood boils from the inside. Shantelle pretends like she wasn't sleeping with Jason the whole time. Brittany fakes a smile before responding.

"I'm pretty tired so I'm about to get a nap in."

The conversation is purposely kept short. Thoughts of their infidelity sit in the back of her mind. She heads to the master bedroom and closes the door. After getting in the bed, Brittany hears a knock. Jason peaks inside.

"Wanna hit up *The Oak Lounge* tonight?"

The Oak Lounge? That's the hottest club in the city. Brittany hasn't been in almost three years. Maybe a date night would do her some good. She agrees to go.

"Sure, that sounds good to me. I'll throw on a dress after my nap."

"Be ready to walk out the door at 8:30." He says while closing the door.

Brittany smiles herself to sleep. Date night will give her a chance to remind Jason of what he's been missing. She's about to throw on a dress tight enough to blow his mind. She definitely knows how to look good. 8:30 P.M. rolls around. Brittany steps out of the bathroom dressed to perfection. Her curves and flawless makeup would put a super model to shame. Even still, Jason's reaction isn't what she expected.

"That dress looks good on you." He says calmly.

That's all she gets out of him. Disappointed, Brittany uses a pocket mirror to do one last make up check. She tries hard to make Jason want her. She decides to be positive and hope it rubs off on him.

"It's been a while since we got to have a date night. I'm excited!" she says.

His demeanor shows there's something he's not telling his wife.

"Oh yeah, about that…."

Shantelle steps out of the guest bedroom dressed ready to hit the night scene as well. Brittany is confused.

"Sorry for taking so long! This dress was hard to get into!" Shantelle smiles while saying.

Jason's jaw drops.

"Shantelle! You look…Amazing. Damn girl!"

Brittany went all out to look good for this fool and this is the response she gets? And Shantelle thinks she's tagging along for the ride?

Make A Choice

Choose what Brittany does next:

Turn to page 146 If Brittany doesn't fight it and lets Shantelle tag along.

Turn to page 148 if Shantelle got Brittany fucked up.

Brittany is tired of being caught up in a love triangle. She responds to Jason with,

"That's good, because so do I."

Jason is surprised to hear her response.

"Wait? Why do you want a divorce?" he asks.

"Because I've been on to ya'll since the day she moved in. I don't have time for this shit!"

Brittany emotionally disconnects herself from her marriage. She storms out and catches an uber to another nearby club. Neither Jason nor Shantelle try to stop her. At the bar, Brittany meets a handsome young man who seems to be very interested in her. The conversation takes her mind off her crumbling marriage.

They eventually exchange numbers. She accepts his offer to go back to his place. She is in no rush to return home after all. Her estranged husband doesn't seem worried as she has no missed calls from him either. While in the middle of sex, police burst down the front door and raid his entire house. Brittany learns the man is a big time drug dealer. He was secretly being monitored by the FBI. It's just plain bad luck that she went to his trap house on the day of the arrest. The man blames the drugs on Brittany to save face. She defends herself by telling the police they just met. They are both detained and receive 8 year prison sentences for intent to sell an illegal substance.

You've reached a dead end.

Make another choice on page 147

"Divorce? What the fuck Jason?"

Brittany can't believe what she heard. Jason emotionally crushes her with his next statement.

"Shantelle made me realize how miserable I've been in our marriage. She makes me happy."

Shantelle feels ashamed. She knows she did her friend dirty.

"Jason, that's enough! I wanted you to tell her but not like this!" she tries to calm him down. He quiets her by covering her mouth before continuing,

"Nah baby she needs to hear this."

Did Brittany just hear that right? Her husband called another woman baby? And what does he mean he's been miserable? For the past nine years Brittany has dedicated her mind, body and soul to this man. She cooks, cleans, gives him sex when he asks for it, balances their checkbooks, and everything. What complaints could this no good ungrateful bastard possibly have? Brittany can't make sense of any of it.

"I didn't realize how unhappy I was until she came along. Brittany we do the same tired ass shit over and over again! We're more like roommates now! This is not what I signed up for!"

Brittany's eyes begin to water. There were no signs of unhappiness until today. Her life collapses with every word he speaks. Jason places his arm around Shantelle.

"To answer your question, yes! Shantelle and I are fucking because we love each other." He says.

Shantelle is embarrassed now that her secret's out. She feels guilty for betraying her best friend. But she's in love with Jason at the same time.

"So that's it? You are walking out of my life after nine years of marriage? Just like that???"

Brittany's tears slowly fall down her cheek.

"You can have the house. Shantelle and I want to look for something a little bigger." Jason speaks in a heartless tone. Brittany shakes her head while he continues.

"In the mean time we plan to get an apartment to save up the money."

Save up the money? Did this fool forget he's a WAREHOUSE MANAGER? He barely makes enough to pay the little bills they have. Brittany tightens her fists out of anger.

Jason and Shantelle rise preparing to leave. He places his wedding ring on the table for Brittany to have.

Before walking off, He says one last thing.

"I'll be more than generous with my alimony payments. Don't thank me. It's the least I can do."

Brittany feels highly offended. She can't be bought out of her marriage. Jason and Shantelle make their way back to his house. Brittany is stranded at 'The Oak Lounge', all alone. Words can't describe how broken she feels.

You are on the right path.

Continue on to page 162

The Best Friend

Alternate Ending #2

Brittany catches a taxi back home. She is furious over being left like that. While pulling up to the driveway, she notices Jason unloading Shantelle's clothing into his truck next to his. He was trying to leave before Brittany had a chance to make it home.

Shantelle avoids eye contact while stuffing the trunk with some of his furniture. Who said he could have the living room couch?

"Where do you think you are going with my couch?" Brittany snaps.

"Come on Brittany I'm letting you have the house. Half the furniture is mine." Jason responds.

Brittany stands before the truck, blocking it in.

Jason and Shantelle hop in the truck ready to escape all the drama. Brittany refuses to move.

"Would you please go in the house? We got a long drive ahead of us."

"Long drive? Where do you think you going with my shit?"

Brittany isn't about to let them leave with anything she didn't approve of him taking. Jason surprises Shantelle by smashing on the gas, forcing Brittany to jump out the way. He takes off down the street disappearing out of the neighborhood. Brittany collapses on the driveway crying her eyes out. For the first time since her mom passed, she feels alone.

A year goes by. Brittany has since found a new lease on life. She quit the airline and found a job as a project manager for a technical consulting firm. She makes a little over six figures. Several weeks after Jason left, she found love again with a well-known doctor. They're taking their relationship slow.

Jason and Shantelle moved two hours outside of town and tried to start a new life together. They were more in lust than love with each other. Shantelle leaves him six months into their relationship. Jason realizes what he had with his Ex-wife. He tries to win Brittany back with passionate speeches about how much he missed her. They all fall on deaf ears.

THE END

Return to page 108 and see if you can find your way to alternate ending #1.

The Work Wife

This story has two alternative endings. See if you can find your way past the dead ends to reach them.

Choose Wisely.

This is a special time in Devon's life. He recently walked the love of his life, Olivia down the aisle. They've become Mr. and Mrs. Henderson just in time for the end of the summer break. They usually receive a lot of time off due to their jobs in the education field. Devon is a mathematics teacher at Bailey High. Olivia works in Human Resources for a college named Newpoint University.

It's a Sunday night. Devon and his wife are celebrating their new life together at the dinner table. He raises his champagne glass to the sky.

"I propose a toast to our future."

"To our future." Olivia responds while texting away on her phone.

Devon gets upset.

"Let's not do this again! Would you please put the phone down??"

Olivia's main problem is she's heavily addicted to social media. This almost drove Devon to call off the wedding. She models online during her spare time and has over 100,000 followers. They consist of mostly men lusting over her pictures. To make matters worse she hides her relationship from the world. Appearing single is a part of her image. Had she not promised to spend less time on the phone during a counseling session they wouldn't have made it this far. Olivia continues to annoy Devon by uploading a picture of her half full wine glass to her account.

"Give me just a second baby, I haven't posted anything since this morning."

Choose what Devon does next:

Turn to page 193 If Devon gives up and heads to his man cave to watch sports.

Turn to page 169 if Devon makes her choose between him and social media.

Devon can't help being attraction to the beautiful stranger. He playfully flirts with her to see where it leads. He justifies the cheating by assuming his wife already has a side dude online.

"It's only Devon to ugly women. For you it's De'Von." He playfully says in a French tone.

The woman lets off a flirty laugh.

"De'Von? Oh really?"

"Not really but it sounds dope doesn't it?" he jokes.

She simply smiles back.

"I can tell we'll get along real well! My name is Angela." She introduces herself.

"I was assigned to help co-teach in your class room"

Devon silently cheers in his head. The semester will be interesting semester to say the least.

Proceed to page 174

Devon's had enough of Olivia's shit. She promised to do whatever it took to make their marriage work back in the counselor's office. Apparently it was a lie.

"I can't do this with you anymore." Devon declares.

"Before we proceed you must make a choice right now. It's either ME or your followers!"

Olivia feels Devon is overreacting. It's just social media after all.

"Why are you so upset? I'm almost done."

Devon feels disrespected.

"You can't understand why your husband is upset his wife is always choosing her damn phone over her marriage? Really?" he responds while frustrated.

"I wasn't intentionally being disrespectful. I'm simply posting a picture while it was on my mind..." She defends herself.

"You posted like 10 pictures today! That shit is always on your mind, that's the problem!"

"Whatever Devon." Olivia returns to entertaining her followers. Devon suddenly loses his desire to celebrate.

He retreats to his man cave. Olivia knows she ruined their celebration dinner. She wishes there was something she could do to get Devon to be more accepting of her hobby. In her mind he's being sensitive.

Devon has a sleeper couch in his man cave. Sheets already cover the mattress. After finishing his night routine, he returns to rest on it. Olivia posts a cryptic message about their fight to her followers.

"Don't ruin other people's happiness just because you can't find your own."

They respond with comments like:

"I know dats right baby."

"Hell yes sexy! I completely agree!"

"This is why you stay away from fuck boys."

With every post comes at least three inboxes messages from men trying to talk to her. She sleeps alone in their bed, giving Devon his space.

The next day he heads to work. He spends most of his time getting his classroom together anticipating the students return next week. While hanging a poster,

Devon is greeted by a beautiful stranger. She walks into his classroom and introduces herself.

"Excuse me. Is your name Devon?" She asks humbly.

Devon can't believe how beautiful she is. Her curves, almond colored eyes, and Mocha skin tone leaves him breathless. Even though she is dressed appropriately, Devon can tell she got a nice shape.

Choose what Devon does next:

Turn to page 199 if Devon tells her to get lost. He's married after all.

Turn to page 198 if Devon accidently lets a DAMN slip out.

Turn to page 168 if Devon starts flirting with her.

Devon sneaks off to his man cave to text Angela.

"Chilling. How about you?" He responds.

"Nothing. Can you believe I made my calculator break? I tried to divide by zero just to see what would happen and it shut off lmao." She texts back.

Devon responds with a series of laughing emojis.

She returns a few of her own.

"I knew you would understand. It's refreshing to talk to someone who finally gets me." she responds.

Devon knows texting her is wrong. But at the same time she makes him feel wanted.

"Well I don't want to keep you from your family. I'll see you Monday!"

Devon spends most of the weekend thinking about Angela. He tried bonding with Olivia by taking her to a fancy restaurant, but she spent more time live streaming her followers than conversing with him. He feels like he married the wrong person.

Monday arrives. Devon is one of the first people to show up to work. This will be his first week co-teaching with Angela. She walks into the class room moments later. The other teachers won't be in for another forty five minutes.

"Hey work hubby!" she says while giving him a warm embrace. Unlike the casual friendly hugs, she presses her whole body against his.

"Hey…." He responds. The sight of Angela's booty got his hormones raging. Maybe she won't be upset if he grabs it? Or maybe she will. There's only one way to find out.

Choose what Devon does next:

Turn to page 178 If Devon slides his hands down to her butt.

Turn to page 204 if Devon keeps his hands above her waist.

Devon and Angela spend the whole day decorating his classroom. They crack jokes that only other math teachers would understand.

"I got a good one!" Devon says.

Angela smiles while looking deep into his eyes.

"What's up?"

"How do you stay warm in an empty room?" he asks.

"Um, go into the corner? Where it is always 90 degrees? Duh!" She responds before lightly punching his arm.

"I heard that one already!"

Devon laughs it off.

"I'll get you one day!" He jokes.

"You goin' learn! I'm the queen of math jokes!"

Devon and Angela recognize how great their chemistry is together. Soon Friday afternoon arrives. They are just about finished for the day.

"It's a shame I'm married. Otherwise I'd ask you out this weekend!" Angela jokes.

Devon responds,

"It's a shame I'm married too. I'd definitely make it a date."

Angela is intrigued.

"Oh yeah? And where would we go?"

"After putting you in a blind fold? We'd pull up to McDonalds."

Angela laughs hysterically. Any joke Devon cracks is ten times funnier in her eyes. Devon can't believe someone who understands his nerdy humor actually exists. He can tell they're going to be friends for life.

Angela gives Devon a hug.

"You know you are my work husband now right?"

Devon pauses for a second. He's never heard the term before.

"Work husband?"

She smiles before heading to the parking lot. Devon's mind runs wild with thoughts of what life would be like if he married her.

Devon heads out, picks up dinner for his wife, and returns home. While at the dinner table, Olivia continues to engage on her social media. Devon gets irritated once again. She notices and puts the phone down.

"So baby, how was work?" she tries sparking up a conversation.

"It was cool. I got assigned a co-teacher in my class room. We spent the day setting it up."

Olivia's phone rings. She can't resist the urge to pick it up. She continues conversing with Devon while scrolling through her timeline.

"That's nice dear. Glad you finally have help."

Night falls. Devon and Olivia sit in the living room with the television on. Olivia goes live on social media, answering questions submitted by her followers. Devon receives a text message from Angela.

"Hey Devon! WYD?"

Devon isn't sure if responding this late is a good idea. It's after dark after all which is disrespectful to his marriage.

Make A Choice

Choose what Devon does next:

Turn to page 172 if Devon goes to his man cave to secretly talk to Angela.

Turn to page 200 if Devon decides to respects his marriage and ignores the text.

Devon is really turned on by Angela. His penis fully erects in his pants. He gently slides his hands down her butt to see how she reacts. Angela smiles while gently removing it.

"Devon...what are you doing..." she asks softly.

He kisses on her neck before backing away.

"Sorry, you just look so good in those jeans. I got carried away."

"You look like a good guy. Who would've guessed you have a naughty side." She jokes.

The other faculty eventually arrives. Devon and Angela get to work. They realize they work better together with the students. Their light hearted math jokes are a hit. Once school lets out, Devon walks Angela to her car.

"You don't really talk about your husband much. Is everything okay at home?" he asks.

She gives him the side eye.

"You don't talk about your wife either."

Devon shakes his head and does the one thing no married man should ever do. He complains about his marital problems to another woman.

"There isn't much to talk about. All she does is post selfies all day. Her followers think she single."

"That's messed up." Angela shakes her head.

"I will never understand why people invest so much energy trying to impress others. They wouldn't care if she died tomorrow."

Devon feels those words in his soul.

"If only she understood that."

"At least she has a good job. My husband is lazy as fuck. He's content with working for 15 dollars an hour."

Devon is appalled.

"Seriously? What kind of shit is that? Why did you marry him?"

Angela looks down,

"It's because we have a son together. I grew up without father. I don't want that for him."

Devon feels sympathy for Angela.

"I would never do you like that."

Angela stares deep into his eyes before getting in her car.

"I'm not ready to go home yet. You wanna hang out for a bit?" she asks while unlocking her passenger door.

Choose what Devon does next:

Turn to page 190 if Devon accepts her invitation. He wants to see how far the rabbit hole goes.

Turn to page 207 if Devon declines her invitation.

Devon gets a Plan B from the pharmacy store. He can't risk his wife finding out. The shame of being caught would be too much to bear.

"I was completely out of line for bringing that addiction out of you. Let's go to the Walgreens and fix this." He says.

"Fix it?" Angela asks.

"Yeah, a Plan B will fix it. I'm sure you don't want your husband finding out you're pregnant by me."

Angela is hesitant.

"I'm sorry Devon. I want to stop this just as much as you do. But I can't bring myself to kill a child."

Devon is shaken to the core. He can't force her to get an abortion. But at the same time his wife can never know about this. Angela promises to keep her mouth shut until the time is right. Eight months go by as the baby grows. Devon continues living his life. Angela feels her stomach rising more each day. She doesn't have the heart to tell her husband the baby might not be his. She allows him to believe otherwise for the time being.

Devon's wife is ready to love him in the best way she can. She uninstalls her social media apps off her phone.

His secret slowly eats him alive. She and Devon are still the best of friends both in and out of the classroom. Devon's feelings for her grow along with his seed. On the ninth month, Angela admits something to Devon in between classes.

"The students are sooo going to hate us for assigning this." He jokes while handing her a stack of papers.

Angela places them on their desk while looking in his eyes. He can tell she wants to talk.

"What Is it Angela?" He asks.

"Devon....I think I'm love with you." She spits out.

Devon is speechless. He is afraid to admit he feels the same way. He also loves his wife. Silence briefly follows before Angela continues.

"You make me feel whole. The universe tells me we're perfect for each other. Even though we are married, I can't help how I feel. I just thought you should know." Angela tells him.

"You're saying this because you're pregnant with my child." He responds.

Devon is emotionally confused.

"I've made up my mind. I'm leaving my husband. Tonight I'm telling him everything…"

Devon tries to change her mind.

"Why? Based on what you tell me, that man loves you. Don't throw it-" Devon is cut off.

"I don't think I will ever find someone I'm as compatible with as you. I know you feel the same."

"I can't just leave my wife Angela." Devon says.

Devon is caught in between a rock and a hard place. Angela isn't for the games. She gives him an ultimatum.

"It looks like you have a decision to make."

Time to make the hard decision. Who does Devon choose?

Turn to page 186 if Devon chooses his wife Olivia.

Turn to page 210 if Devon chooses Angela.

SECRECY AND DECEIT READING TIP:

Alternate endings paths for each story:

The C.E.O. and the office worker:
- Alternate ending #1 path(Happy ending): Choose page 11
- Alternate ending #2 path(The Twist): Choose page 16

The Best Friend:

- Alternate Ending #1 path(Happy ending): Choose pages 99 - 105 - 117
- Alternate Ending #2 path(The Twist): Choose pages 99 - 105 - 120

The Work Wife:

- Alternate Ending #1 path(Happy ending): Choose page 169
- Alternate Ending #2 path(The Twist): Choose pages 193

HIDDEN STORY: IT'S NOT MINE

The story start's here

Nancy knows what she did was wrong. Her husband has no idea their two year old daughter is the result of a night of drunken sex with his best friend Brian. Josh and Brian became best friends after joining a band. Brian and Nancy started off as college sweethearts. She left him due to his career choices after graduation. She did miss his sex and started back sleeping with him behind Josh's back. One day, Josh makes it home after a long shift.

"Hey honey! How was your day?" he asks. Nancy can tell he's exhausted. She smiles.

"It was great! Yours?" She cheerfully responds.

Josh is a good man with a job that makes good money. He provides for her in every way possible. She knows she can't keep this secret from him forever.

Choose what Nancy does next:

Turn to page 233 If Nancy breaks the news that Josh is not the father.

Turn to page 135 if she takes it to the grave.

The Work Wife

Alternate Ending #1

Devon's mind is made up. He isn't willing to leave his wife, especially for Angela. She cheated on her husband with him and got pregnant. She'd only do the same to him.

"I actually have to agree....." He responds.

Angela gets excited. She's ready to start a family with Devon until he finishes his sentence.

"Agree that it's time to fess up to my wife. This whole thing was a mistake."

Angela's eyes water. His words hurt her to the point where she leaves the classroom for the day. Back at home, Devon finds his wife in the kitchen making dinner.

"Hey! How was work?" She asks cheerfully. Devon knows his next words will destroy his marriage. But it has to be said.

"Baby sit down. I have something to tell you."

Noticing the serious tone in his voice, she turns the stove off and takes a seat on the couch. Devon sits beside her and begins letting it out.

"I………………"

He chokes on his words a little. It's hard for him to admit a secret this damaging.

"Just say it." Olivia encourages.

"I stepped out on our marriage."

Olivia's jaw drops. Her once cheerful mood turns sour. A slight tear begins forming. She doesn't like confrontations and finds this situation extremely uncomfortable.

"What?"

A brief silence follows before Devon puts the final nail in the coffin.

"The woman that I cheated with is that coworker I told you about."

"The pregnant woman?" Olivia angrily questions him. Devon spits the secret out.

"Yes. The baby is mine."

Olivia's face drops in her palms.

"BABY I'M SO SOR-" he pleads.

Olivia doesn't allow him to finish that sentence.

"Yes you are. You truly are one sorry motherfucker! How dare you?"

Olivia is beyond angry. Devon tries to calm her down.

"Before we overreact, let's stop and think about this!!"

"Fuck you Devon! I want a divorce!"

His worst nightmare comes to life. She begins packing her things. Devon pleads for her to change her mind. She has nothing left to say to him. A month passes as Angela has her baby. The cheating news tears her husband apart. He leaves only to find out the baby is his. Despite that, he wants nothing to do with her. Angela calls Devon one last time to tell him that he's off the hook. They keep the conversation short and agree to never speak again.

Olivia moves into her sister's house. She finally gets around to hiring a divorce lawyer. After tough negotiations, she and Devon's divorce is finalized. Devon spends most of his time focusing on himself. He deeply regrets all the bad decisions he made. He knows selfishness caused his downfall. The only thing he can do is try not to make the same mistake with the next woman.

Return to page 167 and see if you can find your way to alternate ending #2.

Devon sits in the passenger seat. Angela drives to a secluded area behind the school. The car pulls alongside a few trees, completely hidden from view. The reason she brought Devon there is clear when she begins unbuckling her pants. He watches to see how far she is willing to go.

Angela begins stroking his penis before putting her lips on it. She sucks it slowly like a snow cone on a hot day. Devon enjoys the head. His hands feel all over her breasts. They both pull their pants down. Devon positions himself to have proper thrusting room. Angela slides her vagina onto his penis and begins having sex with him.

Neither cared they were married in that moment. Angela forces her breasts inside Devon's mouth. He grabs her ass passionately with one hand while guiding the curves of her body with the other. Angela turns around burying her head into the dash board. Devon thrusts from behind. It doesn't take long for them to climax.

Shortly after nutting, Devon and Angela regret their actions.

"Devon, there's something I need to tell you…"

Angela tells him with a concerned look.

"What's up?"

"I'm a recovering sex addict. It causes me to make bad choices like this." She answers.

This makes Devon feel horrible. He already broke his vows to his wife. His selfishness also unknowingly took advantage of her problem.

"Being a sex addict isn't such a bad thing." He tries lightening the mood. Angela continues conversing in his lap with no jeans on.

"I don't think you understand. I had my son during my marriage. He's not my husband's biological child."

Those words struck terror throughout Devon's body. He finished inside of Angela's vagina with no condom.

"You on birth control right?" he asks while being afraid of the answer.

"Not exactly…" she responds.

Devon made a huge mistake.

Make A Choice

Choose what Devon does next:

Turn to page 208 if Devon lets his wife know what he's done.

Turn to page 181 if Devon keeps it to himself and prays for the best.

Devon gives up trying to get his wife's attention. He returns to the basement to get a peace of mind. While in deep thought, he questions what he should do about her social media addiction. He decides to trick her by creating a fake account with a random male models picture. This should tell him everything he needs to know. He follows her and sends a D.M. saying,

"Hey beautiful. Are you single?"

Her response shocks him.

"Yea."

Now Devon knows the truth. This pisses him off to no end.

Choose what Devon does next:

Turn to page 196 if Devon confronts his wife.

Turn to page 226 if Devon immediately wants a divorce.

Devon no longer wants anything to do with his cheating wife. He throws her things on the front porch. Olivia uses her phone to livestream the whole confrontation. Her followers talk shit in the comments, saying things like:

"Fuck this dude! That's not how you treat a queen!"

"Why is he putting you out like that? He is a poor excuse for a man!"

One happens to be a Cyber-security Engineer. He traces Olivia's IP Address then informs the police. Olivia gets violent after Devon throws out the last of her clothes. The police pull up seconds later.

Olivia plays the victim crying while running to them. Devon doesn't have time for her Oscar performance. He heads back towards the house. An officer grabs Devon's arm before he could get inside. He snatches it away. The officer takes that as a threat and draws his weapon. This puts Devon in fear for his life. He reaches in his pocket to call 911. Needless to say he never makes that call. The officers fire multiple rounds into Devon's chest, killing him instantly. Olivia cries at the sight of her husband's lifelessly body. She curses at the officers for using unnecessary force. They all get off on a technicality. Olivia uses Devon's story to start a nationwide movement against police brutality.

You've reached a dead end.

Choose a different path on page 197.

Devon storms into the living room. Olivia notices while scrolling a random friend's page. He stands before her with rage in his eyes.

"What's wrong with you?" She pretends to be confused.

Devon reveals himself to be the fake account by showing her his phone. She looks away in shame.

"WHAT THE FUCK OLIVIA? THIS IS WHAT YOU'RE DOING BEHIND MY BACK?"

Olivia burst out in tears.

"I'M SORRY BABY!"

She knows she's been caught.

"Why?" Devon demands.

"Just being stupid! Please forgive me!" Olivia pleads.

Devon wonders if she's truly being sincere. He realizes he doesn't know his wife as well as he thought he did. Olivia tries using sex to make him forget the whole thing. She unbuttons his pants ready to give oral sex. She pulls this card whenever they get into a social media argument. It doesn't work this time.

"You not sucking your way out of this one."

"Fuck Devon! I already apologized! What else do you want me to do?" Olivia angrily asks.

Choose what Devon does next:

Turn to page 194 If Devon doesn't accept her apology.

Turn to page 212 if Devon gives her another chance.

Hey beauty surprises Devon.

"Damn!" He says before regretting his compliment. He then tries to clean it up.

"I am so sorry! I didn't mean to say that out loud!"

Angela is flattered but keeps its professional.

Proceed to page 168

Author's note: This is what you SHOULD do in real life (In a nicer way of course)!

Devon has a classroom to setup. He doesn't have time to converse with new staff members. As beautiful as she is, Devon is married. He can't allow her looks to interfere with his judgment.

"Get lost lady, I'm busy."

The woman is offended and immediately leaves. Other faculty members inform him of who she was. Devon shrugs and goes on with his life. She is reassigned to another department. And just like that, this story is over before it began.

You've reached a dead end.

Choose a different path on page 171.

Devon is married. His wife isn't perfect, but he still made a vow to honor and cherish her. He can't break that for anyone. He decides to ignore the text. Another comes through. The attachment on this message rocks Devon's world.

It is a picture of Angela soaking in the bathtub. Her breasts are exposed with the rest of her body submerged in bubbles. Devon is turned on immediately. His hormones rage for a sexual experience with her. Unbeknownst to him, Olivia walked in to ask if he would help with a full body picture. She silently observes noticing the nude photo.

"DEVON WHO THE FUCK IS THAT?"

He is like a deer caught in headlights. He quickly locks his phone screen.

"Baby I had no idea you were down here!"

Olivia doesn't let him slide.

"Nah uh! Who the fuck is that sending MY HUSBAND nude photos? I know you not cheating on me!"

"It was a wrong number baby! Relax!" He responds.

Olivia snatches Devon's phone then unlocks it. He has no password. She calls the number associated with the photo. Devon knows he's screwed. Angela answers.

"Hello?" she says in a low voice.

"Don't you hello me bitch! Why are you texting my husband? Nude photos at that!" Olivia snarls.

Angela thinks light on her feet.

"Oh my god! I am sooo sorry!I thought I was texting my husband. He recently changed his number!"

Olivia almost buys it, until another angry voice is heard in the background.

"Who you in here lying to? Put your phone on speaker now!" he demands.

The voice is Angela's husband. He was walking by the bathroom when he overheard his wife. Angela shamefully complies by putting Olivia on speaker phone.

"WHO THE FUCK ARE YOU?" He demands to know.

"WATCH YOUR FUCKING MOUTH DUDE! DON'T YOU E-" Devon gets defensive but is cut off by Olivia.

"I'M DEVON'S WIFE! I'M TRYING TO FIGURE OUT WHY THIS WOMAN IS SENDING NAKED TEXT MESSAGES TO HIS PHONE!" Olivia yells back. She has questions of her own for the husband.

He is enraged.

"WHAT THE HELL BITCH?" he yells towards his wife.

Screaming sounds and broken glass follow. Olivia is taken aback at how bad the situation got. The call eventually drops, leaving Devon alone to explain what happened.

The next day, Angela's husband forces her to resign from her job. She ends up running into Devon when he places an order for an extra-large stuffed crust pizza. Angela shows up to his door with it and is greeted by both him and his wife. Olivia has never seen Angela. She has no idea this is the same woman from the phone call. Devon and Angela both pretend to be strangers to keep the peace.

You've reached a dead end.

Choose a different path on page 177.

Nancy knows she's been caught. After making it home, she tells Josh everything. This throws him into a jealous rage. He punches a hole in the wall out of frustration.

"HONEY? WHAT ARE YOU DOING?" she yells fearing for her safety. He blacks out and rushes towards Nancy with the intentions of harming her. She quickly locks herself in the bedroom. He begins trying to break down the door by ramming it. Nancy curls up in a corner petrified of Josh.

"STOP IT JOSH! YOU ARE ACTING LIKE A MANIAC!"

Thoughts of Nancy hooking up with his best friend pushed him beyond the edge. After breaking down the door he begins strangling Nancy. Like a scene out of a horror movie, a man with no face phases through the mirror. The knife he carries is jammed down Josh's throat. Nancy is horrified. Instead of attacking her, He phases back through the mirror never to be seen again. She is never the same after that traumatic experience.

You've reached a dead end.

Choose a different path on page 135.

Devon resists getting a hand full of ass in order to be respectful of his marriage. Knowing how dangerous this can get, he lays down ground rules.

"Look Angela. I think you are very attractive, but I also love my wife. Let's keep this professional."

Devon gets back to work. Angela feels humiliated but knows it's for the better. A few weeks go by. Devon notices Angela spends a lot of quality time with the math professor down the hall. During lunch breaks, she spends alone time with him in his windowless classroom. Something's has to be going on between them. While it's not his problem, he figures he could be a good friend and tell her to slow it down. On a random day he finally speaks his mind.

"Angela, I see you sneaking around with Mr. Banks. Don't forget you're married. You need to reconsider your actions..."

"We are just friends. Are you jealous or something?" she snaps back.

"Jealous? No! I'm looking out for you. Mr. Banks has a wife also.   How do you think this will end?" He responds.

Devon isn't prepared for next thing that comes out of her mouth. She gives him a serious look while closing the door.

"Promise to keep this between us." She asks.

"I promise."

Angela proceeds.

"I was trying to keep this a secret but...Mr. Banks isn't into women."

"What? He has a whole wife? What do you mean he isn't into women?" Devon asks confused.

"I use to be a counselor at my past job. He pays me to tell me how he wants a divorce but doesn't know how to tell her."

Devon is shocked even more with her next comment.

"I probably shouldn't tell you this...but screw it. He actually told me whenever he sleeps with his wife, he pretends she is you."

"What? Oh HELL NO!" Devon is beyond disgusted.

He doesn't know how to handle the news. Now he has to be on the lookout for Mr. Banks at all times. One day Devon catches him staring and confronts him over it. They get into a fight which causes them both to lose their jobs. Mr. Banks was the department head which means he lost the highest paying position there. Angela's secret plan worked. She becomes his replacement. Devon has been set up. Before being escorted off the premises, she whispers something chilling to him.

"Don't take this personal. You two had to go so I could advance."

You've reached a dead end.

Choose a different path on page 173.

Devon knows what he has to do.

"I'm sorry but I can't get in. We both know where that will lead."

Angela is grateful for his maturity.

"You're right. I'm gonna do the right thing and head home. I'll see you tomorrow." She says.

The next day however, she doesn't show up. Devon assumes she overslept and calls her house to check on her. He finds out through Angela's husband that she never came home. A search party tries to locate her. Weeks later, they find her body along with another man by a dirt road thirty miles outside the city limits. When Devon backed out, Angela used her ex-boyfriend as a backup plan. Shortly after murdering her, He shot himself. The motive was jealously over her choice to marry another man.

You've reached a dead end.

Choose a different path on page 180.

Devon knows he has to tell his wife the truth. He won't be able to deny it once the baby is born. After parting ways with Angela he heads home then informs his wife of what transpired. She flips out before moving into a friend's house.

Devon blows her phone up and gets no response. Olivia answers seven days later. She agrees to meet and hear him out. The meeting turns out to be therapeutic for them both. Olivia fesses up to cheating in the past with some of her followers. Devon knows it would be hypocritical to attack her and forgives her.

Olivia no longer has any interest in being exclusive. She walks away after Devon declines her offer to have an open relationship. Angela tells her husband the truth as well. After separating for a week they agree to go to counseling. She manages to convince him to stay with her. She quits teaching in order to start a new chapter in her marriage. Devon is left with nothing.

You've reached a dead end.

Choose a different path on page 192.

SECRECY AND DECEIT READING TIP:

In every story, you will reach a dead end that asks something like:

You've reached a dead end.

Choose a different path on page xxx.

Make a difference choice on the previous page xxx.

This usually means your bad choices led you into a corner with no way out. If you wish to continue the story ALWAYS choose the *'a different path'* option. If you want to see the craziness the other dead end has to offer (Which I strongly encourage), then choose the *'make a different choice'* option. You can always return to the original path once you've read both dead endings.

Devon can't deny their chemistry. They were meant to be deep down.

"You're right. Fuck it, let's do it!" he says optimistically.

"Prove it. Call your wife and tell her right now." She dares him.

Devon nervously holds the phone. He throws caution to the wind and makes the call. After telling his wife that he's fallen for another woman, she tries to get him to change his mind. He hangs up before she gets anywhere.

"Alright now, it's your turn." Devon tells Angela.

She hesitantly calls her husband. He takes the news pretty hard. Angela then heads home to collect her things. She's changed forever when she finds out her husband overdosed on opioids after their conversation. Devon and his wife are no longer on speaking terms and have hired divorce lawyers. Angela informs Devon of her plans to move to another country. She needs to go on a solo healing journey to rediscover herself. She isn't sure when she'll return. Devon is devastated.

Dead End

You've reached a dead end.

Choose a different path on page 183.

Devon isn't about to throw away his commitment to his wife over social media. He hopes she learned from her mistake. They make up afterwards. Devon never truly forgives his wife for cheating on him though. The next day at work he is surprised to see a young woman sitting in his chair.

"May I help you?" He asks.

She smiles.

"Wow! They never told me you'd be this handsome."

She looks young enough to be mistaken for a student.

"Thank you, but class starts in an hour." He says.

"You got it all wrong. My name is Angela. I'm your new co-teacher." She responds.

Devon is confused.

"Lol you're looking at me like I gave you a math problem to solve." She jokes.

Devon and Angela spend most of the day decorating their classroom while trading playful shots at each other. They get along very well.

"So work hubby! When will we get a chance to hang out?" she says.

"Work hubby?" Devon has never heard the term before. Angela laughs.

"Come get a drink with me tonight."

"I can't. I'm married." He hesitates.

Angela's next response shocks him.

"So am I."

Devon is somewhat turned on by the idea.

"Do you really want to hang out with a married man?" He asks.

Angela shuts the door and turns the lights off. She unzips Devon's pants and places his penis inside her mouth. Devon cocks his head back, enjoying the moment before finishing. She swallows his cum and continues sucking on it. She then rises up and turns the lights back on.

"I hope that answers your question."

Devon is hooked. Angela has one more stipulation.

"I expect to be financially compensated when needed. Is that a problem?"

Devon looks at Angela crazy.

"I don't do that trickin' shit! Sorry!"

He tries walking out the door. Angela's next words stop him dead in his tracks."

"Your wife's number is listed as one of your emergency contacts. I have it on speed dial. She doesn't have to find out if you play your role right."

This isn't Angela's first rodeo using men to her benefit.

Choose what Devon does next:

Turn to page 218 If Devon gives in and plays his part in her scheme

Turn to page 231 if Devon refuses to play a role in her manipulation

SECRECY AND DECEIT READING TIP:

The hidden story begins on page 185.

The hidden story begins on page 185.

Devon admits his wrong doing.

"You not the only one cheating! I had oral sex with my coworker today!"

Olivia smirks, signaling she doesn't believe him.

"Boy stop lying. You aren't a piece of shit like-"

"You mean a piece of shit like you?" Devon yells out of anger.

Olivia is hurt by his words. She expresses herself in a way Devon's never seen before.

"Yes. I know I shouldn't cheat but I can't help it. I do truly love you. But I also love the attention social media gives me. When an attractive man gives me his number, I want to see him in real life."

Devon is speechless.

"You're cheating on me and I'm cheating on you. Why are we together?" He asks.

After a deep conversation, Devon and Olivia agree to keep their side pieces. Devon, now no longer in fear of his wife finding out, breaks it off with Angela and searches for other women. Olivia ends up getting pregnant by her side dude. He denies the child as soon as it's born. Olivia turns to Devon expecting him to step up as the father. Devon refuses and files for divorce. He soon notices his check being garnished for child support. Olivia placed him as the father. They both go through a lengthy battle in court which drains Devon's bank account dry of $30,000.

You've reached a dead end.

Choose a different path on page 219.

And just like that, she has Devon by the balls. He doesn't believe her at first until she shows her phone. If his wife finds out their marriage is over. He accepts his role in the situation.

"Okay, so now that we have that established, I'm going to need $1,000 out of your next check to get cute." She says.

Devon is appalled by this request.

"Geez? That's like 1/4 of my entire check? I'll give you $400."

Angela starts dialing his wife's number until Devon stops her.

"WAIT, OKAY! WHATEVER YOU SAY!"

Angela smirks while walking out the door. Her real personality is showing. Unfortunately for Devon, pay day is tomorrow. He has until then to cough up the money. He also has a mortgage to pay. This put him in a financial bind.

After making it home, he notices the door to the master bedroom is closed. Olivia is heard conversing with someone on speaker phone. He slowly opens it to listen in. Olivia continues talking, completely oblivious of him.

"That will be fine. He should be at work by then."

"By when?" Devon asks out of nowhere which surprises Olivia.

"BABY! I MISSED YOU!" She hangs the phone up while saying.

"Don't baby me! Are you cheating again?" Devon is beyond pissed.

"No baby! That was my cousin!" Olivia responds trying to cover her story.

She has always been a terrible liar. But Devon knows his hands aren't clean either. He debates on whether to tell her what he's done.

Choose what Devon does next:

Turn to page 216 If Devon lets her know she's not the only one cheating.

Turn to page 229 if Devon keeps his affair a secret.

Before leaving the house, Devon could tell Olivia was pretending to sleep. Her unlocked phone in her hand reveals the truth. He shows up to work with the money Angela requested. He feels like complete shit when it leaves his hand. She notices and plays with his private area in an attempt to raise his spirits.

They teach their classroom like normal throughout the week. Once Friday arrives, Devon is ready to discuss how he will be reimbursed.

"Let's get a room after work."

Angela responds with an excuse.

"I can't. My family's coming over for the weekend. I promise I got you next time."

Devon can sense something isn't right.

"I told you I expect to be paid by the end of this weekend..."

Angela responds,

"Yeah, it was a last minute thing. Sorry baby."

Devon feels he's being played for a fool. The more she talks, the more everything coming out sounds like complete bullshit.

Choose what Devon does next:

Turn to page 223 If Devon calls her on her bullshit.

Turn to page 222 if Devon feels she is telling the truth.

Devon doesn't believe Angela would lie to him. Besides, his own family has done him that way. He knows what it feels like.

"It's cool. We can wait until next weekend." He casually says.

The weeks that follow, Devon receives more excuses from Angela. He continues paying her, figuring he'd eventually get to reap the benefits. That day never comes. He's finally had enough and plans to confront her until learning she quit the next day. Her false promises cost him over $10,000.

She also disconnected her number so Devon has no way to reach her. Angela has also blocked him on every one of her social media accounts. She played him well.

You've reached a dead end.

Choose a different path on page 221.

The Work Wife

Alternate Ending #2

Devon is aware he's been played and confronts Angela over it.

"ANGELA, STOP LYING! ALL YOU EVER HAVE IS ENDLESS EXCUSES!" He responds in anger

"What? I said I was going to do it! Just not this weekend." She responds calmly.

If Devon lets her off the hook, she'll have another excuse by next week.

"You started this bullshit. We are either fuckin' or you will be paying me back my two grand." The irritation in his voice is heard loud and clear. Angela tries calming him down.

"Devon relax! I got you! We can get a room next weekend! I promise!"

He gives her a chance to follow through on her promise. Another week rolls around as He brings up the room once again. As expected, Angela makes another excuse.

"I'm not feeling well right now."

She hasn't been sick all week. Devon once again pushes it back to the following weekend. She continues making excuses for months on out. He foolishly continues giving money as she promises him a threesome in return.

Devon has finally had enough. He obtains her husband's number through the schools emergency contact list. He then threatens to call him on the spot if Angela doesn't let him fuck after work. She finally agrees to go to a local motel with him. After entering, Devon enters the bathroom to freshen up. Little does he know, Angela quit the school earlier that day. The reason is her husband found work in another state. They are scheduled to jump on a flight first thing in the morning. She figures robbing Devon of his money would help recoup some of their traveling expenses. To Angela's surprise police officers rush out the bathroom and place her in cuffs.

"What's going on? I don't understand!" She cries out.

Devon does his homework and finds out Angela is a wanted woman. She regularly extorts men and vanishes on them at the drop of a dime. After alerting authorities, he agreed to wear a wire.

Angela gets a five year prison sentence for her crimes. Devon tries working things out with his wife until he catches her cheating again. They divorce shortly after. With both toxic women out of his life, he's ready for a fresh start. He quits his teaching and becomes a youth counselor. Interestingly enough, he meets another woman who makes him feel complete. They fall in love and marry shortly after.

Return to page 167 and see if you can find your way to alternate ending #1.

Devon wants a divorce immediately. It's clear social media matters more to her than their marriage.

"I knew this was a mistake." He says while removing his ring.

He places it on the table before silently heading off into the bedroom. Olivia tries to stop him by blocking the door. Devon pushes her aside.

Olivia holds her phone up and presses the power button until it shuts off.

"THERE! THE PHONE IS OFF! ARE YOU HAPPY?"

Olivia finally aware of what her addiction has done to her marriage. Devon is beyond done with her. He packs a few of his clothes and leaves out the door. He books a hotel to live out of for two months. During the first, he meets a young lady working behind the counter named Sarah. They hit it off immediately.

After several dates, Devon finally tells Sarah about his estranged wife. Despite him still being married, she wants to continue dating. One day she invites him over to meet her parents. They drive to an old abandoned wooden house out in a rural part of town.

Sarah walks Devon inside. He notices the house has an eerie vibe to it. The lights are off. Candles are seen in every room. A strange scent fills the air. Five men in long black hoods walk out the shadows to greet him. They each wear a strange anonymous mask.

"What the fuck Sarah?" he asks hesitantly.

Devon realizes he has been led into a cult. Sarah exits the room, leaving Devon alone with the men.

"Welcome to the brotherhood. You have been chosen to be a part of something much greater than yourself."

Devon tries bailing out the front door but can't get it to open.

"Once you walk through that door, there is no escape." A cult member speaks.

Devon backs away slowly only to get held down by more hooded figures. His right arm is injected with a strange green serum before he could fight back. It knocks him out instantly. Devon wakes up chained to a metal beam in the basement. Random cult members brainwash him by not feeding and pushing their teachings on him for months. His mind eventually snaps. He learns to accept their ways. He is freed and helps recruit more members.

You've reached a dead end.

Choose a different path on page 193.

Devon keeps it a secret. He knows telling his wife would do more harm than good. He ends the conversation with a threat.

"I'm sick of this shit Olivia. Cheat on me again and we're finished!"

She immediately feels like shit. He walks off into the comfort of his man cave. Guilt radiates in the back of his mind. He knows he's being a hypocrite. Angela sends him a text out of nowhere.

"Hey sexy. What are you doing?"

Instead of responding instantly, he waits ten minutes to build up the anticipation in her mind. He then texts her back:

"Nothing much."

And then she replies:

"Hubby's check came up short. We need another $1500 to pay a few other bills."

Devon assumes she's crazy for even making that request.

"Let me get this straight. You want another $1500 in addition to the $1,000 I'm already giving you?"

Angela's make him rock hard with her next words.

"I'll let you have your way with me. Nothing will be off limits."

Devon checks his savings balance to verify he has enough to cover it.

"Alright. I got you. But I expect to be repaid by the end of this weekend." He responds.

She responds with a kissing emoji. The situation has turned into more of a business deal. Angela isn't who he thought she was. He never thought in his life he would pay for sex.

You're on the right path.

Proceed to page 220.

Devon refuses to accept the deal. Angela starts dialing his wife's number. Devon snatches the phone out of her hand and slams on to the ground. He then smashes it to pieces with one foot.

"WHAT THE FUCK DO YOU THINK YOU ARE DOING?" he yells aggressively.

"HOW DARE YOU! YOU JUST BROKE MY FUCKING PHONE YOU JACKASS!" she yells back.

Luckily for them, they are on the side of the school that is mostly empty. The classroom cancels outside noise very well. Devon tries to mitigate the situation before somewhere overhears them.

"Keep your voice down! Are you trying to get us fired?"

Angela steps out into the hallway to extract her revenge and yells out,

"HELP! I'M BEING RAPED!!!!"

Devon tries covering her mouth until a campus officer arrives minutes later. He notices Devon being aggressive and takes him down. The authorities are soon notified. Devon gets hauled off to jail. In order to protect the integrity of the workplace, he is terminated the next day.

You've reached a dead end.

Choose a different path on page 215.

There's no point in denying it any further. Tears flow out Nancy's eyes like a waterfall.

"What's wrong honey?" Josh asks concerned.

She sits him down at the table.

"I have something to tell you." Josh hears the trembling in her voice.

"I cheated with Brian...and Dria may not be yours."

Josh stares in disbelief.

"What?"

Nancy balls her eyes out.

"I'm so sorry Josh!" She pleads while begging for forgiveness.

He's beyond hurt.

"Un-fucking-believable! My best friend too??" he says with disappointment in his eyes.

He then grabs a few things and heads out the door. Nancy tries calling his phone but gets sent to voice mail every time. The news was a tough pill to swallow. Josh wants revenge against Brian for ruining his life. After finding him, he shoots at point blank range. Brian dies instantly. The police arrive minutes later. After examining the crime scene, they decide to sentence Josh to prison. Nancy feels guilty for causing him to snap.

You have reached a dead end.

Return to page 185 to make another choice.

"OH MY FUCKING GOD! BITCH WHAT THE FUCK?" Josh yells. They stand before him trying to shield their nude bodies with the bed's comforter.

"WAIT JOSH, GIVE ME A CHANCE TO EXPLAIN!" Brian yells out.

Tears stream down Nancy's face.

Josh punches Brian in a rage as they tussle all over the floor. Nancy yells for them to stop. Josh rises after realizing Brian is too exhausted to continue. Brian knows he lost the fight and tries to hurt him verbally.

"THAT'S WHY I'VE BEEN FUCKIN YO WIFE FOR THE PAST 10 YEARS! ASK WHO YOUR DAUGHTER'S REAL FATHER IS!"

Josh gives Nancy a surprised look.

"What is this fool talking about?" he asks. His suspicions are starting to become reality. She drops to the floor; her body weakened by shame. Despite cheating, she doesn't want her marriage to fall apart.

Josh is disappointed.

"This is how you got me out here looking? Fuck this marriage!" He says before walking off towards the door. She knows if he leaves he's gone for good.

"That's right! Bounce! She been my woman since high school fam!" Brian tries to get under Josh's skin. He is ignored.

Choose what Nancy does next:

Turn to page 238 if Nancy tries to stop him.

Turn to page 93 if Nancy lets him leave.

After visiting the doctor, he informs Nancy that she's pregnant. Brian's the only person she had sex with during the time of conception. How is she going to tell Josh? There is no way he'll forgive her while carrying another man's child.

The time for their dinner date arrives. Josh pulls up to the restaurant dressed to impress. He's open to making things work with Nancy. They both are seated and given menus.

"Hey. How have you been?" he asks.

Choose what Nancy does next:

Turn to page 244 if she hides her pregnancy.

Turn to page 239 if she tells him she's pregnant with his best friend's baby.

Nancy pleads with Josh not to leave her. She quickly blocks the door.

"GET THE FUCK OUT OF MY WAY!" He demands.

Nancy refuses to move a muscle.

A neighbor watching their confrontation while mowing his yard has a low tolerance for abusing women. He races into his house to get a pistol.

Josh manages to shove his way out of the door. Nancy falls on the ground in the process. The neighbor rushes over to Josh pointing his pistol. Fearing Nancy's life is in danger, he shoots Josh in the head. This puts him in a vegetative state. Josh is rushed to the hospital and immediately hooked up to a life support system. Talks of removing it fall on Nancy's hands. After a year passes she accepts he's never going to wake up. She decides it's time to let him rest in peace.

You have reached a dead end.

Return to page 236 to make another choice.

It's Not Mine

The Conclusion

They spend the next hour revisiting the good times. Nancy definitely wants her marriage back. Her demeanor changes once Josh signals for the check. She knows it's time to tell him and decides to be blunt.

"I went to the doctor and found out I'm pregnant."

The announcement takes Josh by surprise.

"Wow…" is all he could muster up.

He knows its Brian's baby without having to ask. The waitress brings the check in the worst timing ever. She also brings out a cupcake per Josh's request.

"Here you are sir." The waitress says while winking unaware of what just transpired. Nancy is surprised.

Josh signals for her to take it back. Nancy snatches it before she has the chance. She pulls out a wedding ring from the inside. Tears flow out of her eyes.

Josh slides the waitress his credit card, ready to leave. Nancy puts the ring on her finger noticing it fits perfectly. She looks Josh dead in the eyes.

"I need you to understand how much I love you! The mistakes I made in the past that are coming back to haunt me. But they won't change how I feel about you."

The pregnancy sealed the deal for Josh. He isn't hearing any of it.

"It's cool Nancy. We had some good times. Now it's time for us to move on."

"Josh, please don't do this..." She responds. Tears continue to flow down her cheeks.

"You had a child on me during our marriage and another one on the way. I have nothing more to say to you..." Josh says while signing the receipt. Nancy is desperate to keep her family together.

"We can still have children." She says. Josh harbors no hard feelings. He rises from the lunch table gives a light hug.

"Thanks for dinner. Be safe on your way home." He says before leaving.

Nine months later she gives birth to a baby boy. Nancy names him after Brian, hoping to motivate him to be more active in his life. Brian wants a relationship with her but is shut down. She moves forward, not backwards.

Josh redirects his focus into his career. He re-enrolls in college and obtains his master's degree. This pays off big time as Josh secures a half a million dollar salary via his own consultation business. He treats himself to a 4,000 square foot house in a gated community. He eventually marries a high powered attorney.

Nancy barely gets by with her job as a call center agent. Brian's $150 dollar child support payments barely pay a bill. She eventually falls in love with a mechanic. He accepts her children as his own and proposes after two months of dating. They get married and live a happy life.

Hidden Story Ending

The End

SECRECY AND DECEIT READING TIP:

Unlike the main three, this story only has one ending. Reaching this point means you've most likely completed the entire book. I can't thank you enough for taking the time to finish my master piece. Be sure to read all of the dead ends.

Until next time.

-Willie James

Nancy isn't about to ruin her marriage a second time. She plans to have sex with Josh and pretend he's the father. After dinner, she invites him back home. He shows up, ready to have a romantic evening with her. They hear a knock on the door while relaxing on the couch. It's after 9 pm which is too late for a visitor. Josh, assuming its Brian, answers ready for another fight. He opens the door to see a man wearing a creepy mask standing before him.

"It's late. What do you want?" he asks.

The man tilts his head, giving off a disturbing vibe.

"Whatever! Get lost kid!" he yells before slamming the door.

Nancy peeps out the blinds and notices the creepy figure slowly walking to the middle of street. He stares at their house without moving a muscle.

"I think we should call the police." she says while panicking.

Josh opens the door ready to fight with the stranger, only to see him gone. Nancy is confused peeping through the blinds again.

"Wait, He was just standing there not even five minutes ago!" she says.

"That was probably some kid who got bored and moved on to another house." Josh says confidently. He pulls Nancy back to the couch and begins feeling all over her. He then slowly removes her panties. Seconds later, another knock on the door is heard. Josh frustratingly pulls up his pants.

"Got damn kids!" he yells while flinging the door open. He stares face to face with the creepy man in a mask.

"Look, didn't I tell your ass to get lost?"

The creep says nothing.

"Beat it kid before I call the cops!" Josh demands.

He notices one of the creep's hands is kept behind his back. The stranger quickly pulls out a knife and stabs Josh in the neck. He stumbles backwards into the living room in shock while trying to pull the knife out. Too much blood is lost. He falls lifeless to the floor. The creep grabs the knife then walks in a slow killer life fashion towards Nancy. She races into the bathroom, slamming the door shut. She panics, fearing the killer could break the door down any second. She hears nothing but silence.

Five minutes later, she opens the door slightly to see what's going on. Both Josh and the crazy intruder are nowhere to be found. She uses the opportunity to bolt to the police station. Once there, she learns a forty year old mental patient had escaped an asylum the night before. He was last seen in their area. They spend months searching for him hoping it will lead to the recovery of Josh's body. The leads never get them anywhere. Nancy develops P.T.S.D. fearing the masked man will return for her one day.

You have reached a dead end.

Return to page 237 to make another choice.